The characters in this book are imaginary.
Their names have no relation to those of actual people
living or dead—except by coincidence.

First published in the United Kingdom 2021.
Copyright © Leanne Hamilton.
All rights reserved.

A catalogue record of this book is available from the British Library.

ISBN 978-1-7398258-1-2

Cover © Leanne Hamilton

Published by © Newford Publishing

~ Shards of Porcelain ~

Shards
of
Porcelain

---

by Leanne Hamilton

Introduction

This was it. The final song of the band's farewell gig. The grand finale as they played their biggest hit song to date. The band had worked tirelessly together in this line-up for the past six years and had faced a multitude of ups and downs during their career and tonight was time for the five bandmates, their managers and their engineer to go their separate ways. The atmosphere of the audience looked electric but as young keyboard player, Liz, scanned the stage looking at her bandmates, it was a totally different story altogether.

Liz was exhausted and felt so much older than her 21 years. She could not remember the last time she had eaten or slept properly and her weight had plummeted. The custom-made cat suit that once hugged her petite figure now hung loosely on her. Her bandmates also looked frazzled. The only one who seemed to be holding it all together was her recently estranged boyfriend and lead guitarist, Moose. But then, that was Moose. He had this tough guy image to uphold and would rarely show any kind of emotion in front of anyone. One of the most difficult decisions Liz had had to make in her short life was to break up with Moose but she felt she had no other choice. He had proposed to her just two weeks previously but she had declined as she had planned to move back home to Scotland where her eldest brother Harry, a well-respected medical consultant, had offered her refuge and had managed to source help for her as she battled her anorexia and other demons that were haunting her. She had also planned to go to university to continue her studies while she still had youth on her side. Liz loved Moose far more than she could put into words but she had to get away for both their sakes as she knew she would never survive her demons if she stayed in the U.S., where too many of the wrong people knew her. She also did not want to be a burden on Moose. He just did not understand her decision and had barely looked in her direction since they had split. Liz looked at the rest of her bandmates. Their lead singer and younger brother of Moose, Angel, whom she looked on as a big brother, looked emaciated and ill. His once athletic physique was now ravaged by drink and drugs, yet he still carried on being the perfect showman that he was for the sake of the audience. Their drummer, Carlos (Carl), was also struggling with a severe drink and drug problem. For almost a year now, the two friends had these problems that had spiralled out of control and they seemed to hold onto each other. As a result, they had pulled each other down into a predicament that was like quicksand.

Again, Carl's deteriorating health was unknown to most of the audience as he carried on playing the drums to a very high standard despite being absolutely wasted on stage. Ronnie, their bass player, had cried for almost the entire gig as his thoughts were elsewhere. Their engineer, Debbie (Ronnie's beautiful wife), had recently given birth to their daughter, Caitlin, three months prematurely. Both mother and baby were critically ill in hospital so it was understandable that Ronnie did not want to be there. Still, he had the fans' best interests at heart and had turned up to play to the best of his ability one last time. Liz had other worries to deal with outwith the band too. Her father, who helped manage them, was unable to be there that night as he had to fly home to Scotland in an emergency. Another of Liz's older brothers, Hugh, had been involved in a serious multi-vehicle accident that had left him critically ill, in a coma and doctors were unable to say whether or not he would survive due to extensive internal bleeding. Throughout the gig, Liz kept catching eye contact with an older lady in the audience. She was a maternal-looking lady in her fifties and she looked at Liz with pity in her eyes as she knew fine what was really happening on stage. "If those were my kids, I would be worried sick," Liz heard her say to a younger woman, possibly her daughter, during a break in the music. Liz could not control her tears as she had been crying since long before the start of the gig and for days running up to it. There was no point in her even trying to do her make-up tonight as it would have just run straight off.

The end of the gig was now upon the band as all the members played the massive outro of their instruments and finishing in unison to a massive, roaring cheer from the audience with many of the devotees in tears. "Thank you so much, beautiful people," slurred Angel as he held onto Moose's shoulder for support while Moose continued to prop him up. "Thank you, so much, from all of us for being there for us and making our band what we are. Love you all. Please take good care, stay safe and *KEEP ON ROCKIN'. GOOD NIGHT AND GOD BLESS.*"

Moose and Ronnie helped Angel backstage, where he immediately blacked out. Liz took Carl by the arm and allowed him to steady himself as they walked awkwardly backstage. Carl just made it to the toilet, where he projectile vomited before staggering out and collapsing on the floor. Meanwhile, Ronnie continued to cry quietly to himself.

Paramedics burst through the back door, took details from band manager Jose Martinez, also known as Papa Joe, (Carl's father) and Carl was rushed to hospital. Moose put a strong arm around Ronnie's shoulders and guided him out the back door, avoiding as many eyes and cameras as possible, to take him to hospital to reunite him with Debbie and Baby Caitlin as he had promised. That just left Liz with Angel, who was still unconscious on the floor. A steward managed to get him to stir enough so that he and a colleague could take an arm each and carry him onto the tour bus while Liz followed behind carrying Angel's treasured guitar.

During the drive home, Liz's thoughts were rushing through her head at a million miles an hour: her beloved Moose that she had lost forever, Ronnie and his sick wife and baby, Carl and Angel who both had their demons to contend with and her brother Hugh, whom she prayed would continue to fight for his life and win.

As soon as they arrived home, Danny the burly coach driver and engineer carried Angel, who was over six feet tall, off the bus and into their mansion as though he were a small child and laid him, gently, on the only bed left. The magnificent house that had been the bandmates' home for the past four years had already been sold and was almost cleared out for the new residents who were due to move in the following week. "Can I take you anywhere, love?" asked Danny. "No thanks, darling," replied Liz. "I'm going to stay with Angel." "As long as you're sure," said Danny as he reluctantly headed for the door.

Liz put $100 into Danny's shirt pocket and hugged him to say thank you for helping as she wished him all the very best for the future. She had no strength left to even speak anymore. Liz lay on the bed beside Angel and cuddled up to him for heat as she could hear the rain lashing heavily on the window and the howling wind outside. As tired as Liz was, she was too afraid to go to sleep as she was worried about Angel's worsening condition. She had no idea what kind of concoction of alcohol and narcotics he and Carl had taken prior to the gig, his breathing was now very shallow and his lips and hands were tinged blue. Liz held Angel's cold hand as she called 911, willing him to keep breathing. The paramedics were there within minutes and Liz stayed with Angel at the hospital until the doctors took him away for his treatment. She felt helpless but there was nothing more she could do for the gentle soul who had held her hand and supported her ever since she had joined the band. She couldn't wait any longer as she had to catch her flight back home. All she could do was hope that Angel would come out of this and follow the instructions that she had left him. "I'm so sorry, my dear Angel," Liz thought as she wept quietly. "Please keep fighting this." Liz was almost too exhausted to walk or keep her eyes open anymore as she got into a waiting cab and made her way to her father's house. This was the less glamorous side of being a rock star.

Chapter 1:
Amber's Rock Investigation

Amber Groves arrives early for her induction for her new radio presenter job at Golden Plus FM—a station specialising in music intended for the 40-plus age-groups.

Having worked in journalism since leaving school, it had been her dream to do this job, and now it was finally hers. This particular radio station specialises in the type of music that she was brought up listening to, which made it even better. Not only is Amber a massive fan of most of the music being played, for someone so young, she has a wealth of knowledge of the history of the music and of the artists. Her induction is complete, she is ready to go on-air for the very first time as a radio presenter at 12 p.m. Not everyone is happy for Amber. Aged just 24, she is the youngest presenter by far ever to be employed there and she faces a lot of criticism and heckling from her fellow presenters, other staff members and listeners alike. Some say she is far too young, inexperienced and dumb to work there, while others accuse her of doing sexual favours for senior management in order to get the job in the first place. Seriously? These are comments coming from adults in their forties and fifties. Surely this kind of bitchiness is supposed to be left in your school playground? Obviously not in this industry!

Amber's first show goes very well indeed. It is an absolute buzz being on-air with the majority of the listeners texting in to congratulate her and welcome her to her brand new slot and to tell her what a fine job she is doing. Of course, there are one or two nasty and lewd texts from listeners but, with Amber being a young female, that was to be expected. If Amber has learned anything in her time as a journalist, it is that, no matter how good you are, you are never going to please everyone. Still, she feels like a natural on-air as she chats with listeners on the phone and via text message while she plays all the favourite hit songs from the 1980s to the early naughties. The studio phone rings and a male listener is put through from switchboard to speak to Amber off-air.

"Hello, Amber," says the man. "My name is Derek and I am general manager at Moonlight Laundry Services. My team and I are regular listeners to this slot."

"Hello, Derek," replies Amber. "Thank you for calling. What can we do for you?"

"First of all," says Derek, "congratulations on the new job. My colleagues and I at the office are loving your work. I am also calling because I have an idea for a challenge for your show."

"Sounds interesting," enthuses Amber. "I am always open to suggestions from listeners on how I can improve my show and give you guys a better listening experience. What is your suggestion?"

"Do you know a band called Hell Freeze?" asks Derek.

"Yes," exclaims Amber, excitedly. "My parents are

massive fans of their work and they passed their great taste onto me. My mom always had a monster crush on Angel and it is still my dad's ambition to have a sparring match with Moose. Also, Liz was my first ever girl crush."

"WOW," gasps Derek. "I didn't expect that! I can tell by listening to your show that you are a fountain of knowledge when it comes to music of that era and it seems you and I are reading off the same song sheet. Sorry, no pun intended there! Anyway, here is my suggestion. How about you take some time out and investigate how to reunite this great band? They were untouchable for five years, they had hit song after hit song and were never off our television screens and radio airwaves then, *POOF!*, they suddenly vanished into thin air never to be seen nor heard of again. There is no information, whatsoever, on the band members. They can't be found on Google, nor do any of them have Wikipedia pages. They all seem to have disappeared like tiny shards of porcelain."

"Goodness," gasps Amber. "It sounds like an interesting project but it's how to get started. We don't even know if the band members are still alive!"

"That's your challenge," replies Derek. "They are an older band who have been out of the public eye for twenty years but I already have one to start you off. Carl Martinez, the drummer, is doing a book signing at Candy's book store this coming Friday at 10 a.m. He has written a book about his time with the band and about all their ups and downs. Why not publicise your investigation when you are on air? Other listeners may be able to elaborate on the information I have given you. Also, get along to Candy's and try to get a one-to-one chat with Carl himself? I'm sure he would be more than happy to talk to you and if he is that down on his luck, he may jump at the chance to reunite with his band or even reform."

"This is so exciting," cries Amber. "Derek, thank you so much. I am taking your advice on board and work starts right now!"

"Cheers, Amber," replies Derek. "All the very best with the investigation. We'll look forward to seeing it all unfold."

Amber is beside herself with excitement. She loved this band's work when she was growing up; now she could be the one to reunite them and, possibly, get them to play together again. This is Amber's first major operation as a radio presenter and she plans to endeavour to make it a success.

Chapter 2:
Angelo

Having been homeless for several years now, Angelo faces another night sleeping on the streets. The saving grace is that it is not cold and it is dry. Tonight must be student night as the streets are awash with young people all dressed up and travelling between the various bars and night clubs. Angelo finds a sheltered corner out of sight of as many people as possible so he can settle down to sleep for the night. He is just drifting off when he is disturbed by what sounds like people arguing. In the distance, he can hear what sounds like two young girls shouting, pleading to be left alone and crying for help. Angelo gets up and walks briskly to where he thought he heard the disturbance. Down the nearby alley is a group of people comprising of two young girls, who can't be any more than sixteen years old, and five men aged from their early twenties to late thirties. The guys are clearly harassing the young girls and trying to take them somewhere against their will.

"Please stop," pleads one of the girls. "We don't want to go."

"You're coming with us whether you like it or not," jeers one of the men as the rest of them laugh.

"*HEY*, they said they do not want to go with you. Leave them alone! You heard me. Now fuck of," shouts Angelo in broken English.

"Who are you, old man?" scoffs another of the men. "Step away before you get hurt, granddad."

"Granddad is gonna do you a bloody mischief, you little prick," Angelo thinks to himself.

The biggest of the men runs towards Angelo and is met with a swift kick to the groin followed by an elbow strike to the back of the head. Angelo turns sharply to another man who is charging at him and grabs him by the throat before finishing him off with a vicious left hook. Another of the men jumps on Angelo from behind but is thrown head over heels, landing on the base of his back and shattering his spine. The fall leaves the man screaming in agony and unable to move. Angelo looks at the other two men and smiles through his long, matted, grey beard. "It's OK, big guy," stammers one of them as they both run off. "We don't want any trouble. We'll be on our way. Peace out."

The two young girls watch in awe the whole time, barely able to believe their own eyes. What did they just see?

Angelo asks in his broken English: "Are you girls alright?" The girls nod as they cry with relief, knowing they are now safe. Angelo flags down a cab, speaks briefly to the driver and beckons the girls over. Still crying and very shaken, they thank Angelo and get into the cab.

Angelo settles back down into his corner, hoping that would be the last of the drama for that night. A little while later, the same cab driver pulls up to the kerb in front of Angelo and points at him. A tall well-dressed man gets out of the passenger seat, strides over to Angelo and crouches down in front of him. "Hey there, my good man," he says. "I just want to thank you very much for what you did for my daughter and her friend tonight. According to my girl, you were truly magnificent."

"Aw, it was a nothing," replies Angelo.

"Don't be so modest, my friend," says the man as he places a hand on Angelo's shoulder. "Come on. Let's get you out of here in case those guys come back with reinforcements."

The man checks Angelo into the best hotel he can find as he thanks him profusely for his trouble before bidding him goodbye. At least now he could clean himself up and he had a bed for the night. Definitely no more drama tonight. Angelo could finally get some peace.

Angelo wakes up from another broken sleep, his knuckles bruised from his night of law enforcing on the city streets. He has had yet another nightmare during the brief time he had managed to sleep, the same recurring one that has haunted him for many years now. He had done a really evil, unspeakably wrong thing in his younger days and he guessed that having to sleep on the streets was his punishment. Despite being fully awake, Angelo can still hear all the voices from his nightmare. A young woman screams in agony and cries for mercy as she begs to be set free. He can hear his mother's voice: "Angelo, how could you?" she sobs in Italian.

He hears his brother's deep, gruff voice also in Italian: "You vile piece of shit. You had better pray that I never get my hands on you."

An old work colleague threatens, in a broad Scottish Glaswegian accent: "You're dead, son."

Angelo observes the city streets from the third-floor hotel room window. It is 4.45 a.m and a petite woman with cropped, blonde hair is out for her early morning run as he has seen her do regularly for several years now. He would know that running gait anywhere but he never acknowledges her or makes his presence known to her. He wouldn't dare. Angelo imagines she is working nearby as he often sees her going about business in her tailored clothes, sometimes biker gear. Still, he is glad she seems to be doing well for herself.

"Come on, guys, you're doing a terrific job. One final sprint finish and we're done. Keep moving forward. Let's go!" Another voice and figure that Angelo knows too well. The old school bootcamp instructor with the deep, rough voice is built like a tank and still looks very youthful despite now being in his sixties. This guy really knows his stuff and could put people less than half his age to shame. He appears to be doing well in his career as a personal trainer and instructor. He is also probably married with a family of his own and, possibly, grandchildren too now. Anyway, that is another bridge that was burned long ago.

Angelo checks out and heads back onto the streets, not even bothering to wait for breakfast. He thinks of his mother, whom he has not seen nor spoken to in twenty years and wonders if she is still alive. He spots that fit, blonde woman again. She is now dressed in a tailored trouser suit and is deep in a telephone conversation. All the while, she seems to be looking in his direction. If only he could talk to her.

The blonde woman greets the person on the other side of the phone and Angelo can just hear her unmistakable deep voice and broad Scottish Glaswegian accent. "Hiya, sweetheart...I'm just phoning to see how you are. Yes, I am fine. Still as busy as ever. Sorry, hun, I've not seen or heard anything. Are we still on for Tuesday? Great, see you then. Love you loads. Bye."

Angelo's daydream is broken by a woman's high-pitched scream. The woman at the other side of the road is being attacked by two men. "Fuck it," mutters Angelo to himself. "I can take them both."

"HEY!" shouts Angelo as he dodges the traffic to get to the two attackers. He catches one of the guys with an uppercut that sends him flying, knocking him unconscious. Then he floors the other one with a flying kick to the stomach as he goes for a counter-attack. The young man lies doubled up in pain on the ground, still clutching the woman's purse. Angelo lands one final kick to the guy's stomach as he lets go of the purse. Both of the young guys clamber to their feet and run off as fast as their legs can carry them.

"Thank you so much, mister," says the woman, relieved, as Angelo returns her purse to her.

"Itsa quite alrighta ma'am," smiles Angelo. "It was a nothing. You shoulda be safe now."

The woman watches as the mysterious, homeless immigrant walks smartly away. Who is that? She knows him from somewhere but she cannot, for the life of her, place him. She tells her manager about her attack as soon as she arrives at the office. "June, if you are that traumatised you can go home," says her manager. "We can take care of things here."

"Honestly, Eddie, I'm fine," replies June. "That homeless man who came to my rescue, though. Good God, he was something else! He was like a bloody ninja the way he took on those guys single-handedly then he walked away before I could even offer him a reward, very modest about it all."

"It sounds like you're talking about Old Angelo, June," replies Eddie.

June: "Angelo?"

"Yeah," sighs Eddie. "He is a good guy but he is down on his luck but he never asks anyone for anything. It certainly wouldn't be the first time he has put the local riff-raff in their place, that's for sure!"

As Angelo sits resting at his usual place, he sees somebody else he recognises. He puts his head down and pretends to be asleep as the street sweeper walks past him de-littering the pavements, whistling happily as he goes. He then hears the unmistakeable Scottish highlander's accent: "There you go, pal," whispers the street sweeper. "In case you've not eaten today."

Unknown to the kind-hearted street sweeper, Angelo recognises him from a former life. Apart from being older now, he hasn't changed at all. The tall, slender gentleman with the red, spiky hair, which is now greying slightly looks just as he did all those years ago and, of course, he has the same warm, caring nature. Still, Angelo does not dare to reach out, preferring to stay invisible and silent to all who knew him in that past life. He opens an eye slightly to see that the street sweeper has left yet another packet of sandwiches for him. One day he would thank him properly for his kindness.

Angelo gets up and goes for a walk around the streets to stop himself from seizing up. He walks past the electrical shop and happens to look in at the televisions and he thinks he sees a face he recognises on one of the wide screens. He walks in to investigate.

Presenter: "Joining us in the studio today is music producer and DJ Liz McLarnon, formerly of rock band Hell Freeze, promoting her brand new hit single featuring the voice of up-coming young vocalist, Zayn Thomas. Welcome, Liz. Thank you for joining us this morning."

Liz: "Thank you for having me. It's a pleasure to be here."

Even after all her years living here in the States, Liz's Scottish Glaswegian accent is still very apparent, although she had to try her best to thin it down in order to be understood by her friends and acquaintances of her new home. As with the kind street sweeper who would often leave food for Angelo, her fellow Scots would have been proud.

Presenter: "How does it feel to be back after all this time? We've not heard from either you or your bandmates for twenty years."

Liz: "It really is an honour. It was nerve-wracking after such a long break from the industry but as long as people are enjoying what I do as an artist and other artists are willing to work with me, that's good enough for me. I appreciate everyone's loyalty and kindness and I can't thank them enough. Zayn and all the other artists I have worked with over the years have been absolute stars."

Angelo is approached by a sales assistant. "I'm really sorry, sir, you cannot be in here," she says.

"Sorry, ma'am," replies Angelo in perfect English. "I'll just be on my way. *Aaww,* shit!"

The assistant gasps and her eyes widen. "Please take all the time you need, sir," she whispers to him.

Angelo, in his broken English: "Thank you so much, ma'am."

The store manager, angry at the assistant, calls her over. "What the Hell are you doing, Eva?" he asks. "You know we don't allow that type in here."

Assistant: "Jon, I'm sure that's Angel Mancini from the band Hell Freeze. It's the eyes and I would know the voice anywhere! He is pretending he can't speak English very well. I really hope it's not him, though, because he has fallen on some real hard times if it is."

Jon watches as Angelo continues to listen to what Liz McLarnon has to say in the interview.

Presenter: "What about your former bandmates, Liz? Do you see or hear from anyone? It is also understood that you were blamed for the band's demise."

Liz: "Our final year together was an extremely difficult time for all of us as we were all exhausted, sick and at breaking point. Yes, I took the blame for breaking up the band but I was very young and too ill to fight the media. The guys could have taken on another keyboard player had it been technically feasible for them to continue but it just wasn't. There were so many problems within the band in the year running up to the break-up and every one of us had issues, which was no wonder as we had worked constantly against the grind for five years solid with no breaks. I was struggling with anorexia, Carl and Angel both had problems with drink and drugs and Ronnie's wife and newborn baby girl were seriously ill. Ronnie was, understandably, sick with the stress of everything that was going on. The only one of us who seemed to be powering through it all was Moose. But then, you never could tell with Moose because of that tough exterior of his. I've not seen or heard from any of my bandmates since we parted ways all those years ago. I would love to see them again but I doubt it will ever happen. After all, I looked on those guys and Debbie as my family, not just work colleagues."

Presenter: "I am sure the audience at home would like to hear more about your relationship with your bandmates. Are you willing to share?"

Liz chuckles as she remembers her audition. "I was only fifteen years old when I joined the band," she smiles. "It was not a pretty sight either as I had turned up to my audition still in my uniform as our manager, Papa Joe, had picked me up straight after school after he had heard me play the piano while my classmates sang as he recorded a Christmas jingle for his radio station. He asked me if I played keyboard as his son and his friends were looking for somebody with good technical knowledge, to which I replied that I preferred keyboard to piano and that I would try my best. With my long, afro-ginger hair, puppy fat and no make-up I was no beauty like Britney Spears! I was just as taken aback when I met them as I was expecting a group of young, teenaged boys full of carry-on rather than tough, thirty-something, leather-clad, long-haired rockers because Papa Joe had spoken about 'my boy and his pals' throughout the car journey!"

Everyone laughs at this, including Angelo. Still, he holds his breath. Is Liz about to spill the beans and reveal some real ugly truths?"

Presenter: "Aw, Liz, you have to tell us about THAT look. You became quite the trend-setter as all the teenaged and twenty-something girls AND boys wanted a 'Liz' hair-do and biker gear."

Liz: "I was often dubbed an 'ugly duckling' in comparison to my pin-up counterparts. The final straw was when I started doing my bit as a backing vocalist and somebody commented that 'the chubby little girl should come out from behind the keyboard kit'. I knew something had to change. Moose and his colleague, Marco Pieraccini of Trojans' Fitness Gym, took me under their wings so that I could trim down and get fit safely. Then I got a well-needed make-over from Ronnie's model wife, Debbie. Out went the ginger fro, baggy jeans and sweaters and in came the shaven, peroxide hair, make-up, catsuits, tight jeans and bandage dresses. It made me so much more confident about being on stage and, later, stepping out with the gorgeous Moose. I am also about to shatter the band's image here."

"Shit," Angelo thinks to himself. "Here we go."

Liz: "OK, here goes. The guys had themselves down

as Hellraisers with their on-stage antics but they were nothing but perfect gentlemen when it came to me. OK, they were less than impressed when they first saw me and I couldn't blame them. Moose wanted to sign me up as soon as he heard me perform my first track and Angel backed him up, as did Ronnie. Carl was sceptical because I was so young and he felt I would have been a hindrance, which I couldn't blame him for. After all, it was his father's business."

Presenter: "What about your relationship with Moose? You were quite the power couple back in the day despite the vast age difference and you still speak very fondly of him."

Liz: "I was nineteen years old and Moose was 39 when we started dating. OK, I was very young and inexperienced but, somehow, it worked. It was actually me that gunned for Moose as I had really fancied him for such a long time. He treated me like a queen while we were together and he is definitely one in a million. I really hope he is doing well now, wherever he is. The other guys reacted differently when our relationship came to light. Angel was furious because he had his brother down as a skirt chaser and he didn't want to see me get hurt, the absolute darling that he is."

Angelo smiles and he can feel himself blush under his long beard.

Liz continues: "Carl thought it was hilarious and Ronnie and his wife Debbie wished us well. Debbie, Papa Joe and the four guys protected me from so much while I was with them. I really am a lucky woman who can say she experienced so many wonderful things so young. I just hope all my bandmates and associates are all doing well now. The only one of us that I know of who had work to go to in the music business was Angel. He managed to secure a record deal, he had modelling contracts and he was writing music for various big-budget movies due to be released around that time. He is probably happily retired and enjoying life now."

"Aw man you couldn't be further from the truth, baby," Angelo says quietly as he hangs his head.

Presenter: "Liz, thank you so much. For the audience watching at home, here is Liz McLarnon's new hit single 'Reflections' featuring Zayn Thomas. Enjoy."

"WOW," Angelo thinks to himself. "She didn't say anything. At least not what I thought she would say. 'An absolute darling'? I didn't expect that AT ALL! She even defended Moose. At least she doesn't seem bitter about anything."

Angelo nods and mouths "Grazie" to the kind female assistant and her manager as he leaves the shop, definitely feeling a million times better having heard Liz speak. Jon the manager runs after him. "Excuse me, sir," says Jon. "We're in for a cold snap tonight so please accept these passes for the nearby hotel. You will, at least, have a bed and some food for a couple of nights."

"Grazie, signore," smiles Angelo.

Jon goes back to report to Eva. "That's Angel alright," he says. "That fake Italian accent is fooling no bugger. I wonder what happened to him?"

"I suppose that's what happens when you leave the limelight," says Eva. "I just hope something turns up for him before it's too late."

Chapter 3:
Amber's Appeal

Amber is back on air at Golden Plus FM, excited about listener Derek's suggestion that she has decided to follow through. She plays one of Hell Freeze's many hit songs and her in-box goes wild as so many listeners text in gushing about the band and how they are very sorely missed.

"Good afternoon, everyone," Amber greets her audience. "You are listening to Lunchtime With Amber on Golden Plus FM. Thank you for all your text messages and I will definitely make sure I have more from Hell Freeze for you later on in the show and in the future."

"Whatever happened to Hell Freeze?" Amber asks her audience. "They were a rock band of their generation who had it all: the looks, the musical talent and the genius songwriting. It just doesn't seem right that they disappear into thin air without warning or any reason. Reading through your text messages, it seems I am not the only one who would love to see this fantastic band re-united. Thank you so much to Derek from Moonlight Laundry Services who has phoned in. He tells me that Carl Martinez, the band's drummer, is doing a book signing at Candy's Book Store this coming Friday at 10 a.m. Please be sure to call in and buy a book from him. It would be an invaluable gift for any Hell Freeze fan. If anyone else has any information about the whereabouts of the other band members, please feel free to call the station and we will chat off-air."

Amber puts some songs on the loop and notices she has a call coming through to the studio from switchboard. "Good afternoon," Amber says as she answers her phone. "Thank you for calling Golden Plus FM. You are speaking with Amber. Who am I speaking to?"

"Hello, Amber," replies the male caller with a European accent. "My name is Lukas Breitner and I own Trojans' Fitness Gym in town. I have some information for you with regards to your project."

"We are off-air, Lukas," assures Amber. "Please tell me what you know."

"The lead guitarist from Hell Freeze, Moose, is a long-term friend of mine," Lukas informs her. "He works for me as a gym instructor and personal trainer and goes by his real name, Mario Mancini, these days. He is a workaholic who practically lives in my establishment. When he's not working, he's working out and he is so focused on work that he will have no idea that this investigation of yours is going on. It would do him a world of good to get away from here for a bit if you want to come in and chat to him."

"Thank you so much for that information, Lukas," enthuses Amber. "It is greatly appreciated. I am actually a member of your gym but, unfortunately, I don't have the discipline that Moose, sorry, Mario does. Our chat has definitely given me the motivation to at least put my sneakers on."

They both laugh. "You are very welcome, Amber," says Lukas. "Like I say, Mario is in pretty much all the time so please call in any time. If he's not in the gym, somebody will be able to tell you where he is. All the very best with the rest of your investigation. Goodbye, Amber. I'll see you in the gym now that you have your mojo back."

"Goodbye, Lukas," says Amber. "Thank you so much and I will see you very soon."

Just as Amber hangs up the phone, she notices another call waiting. She picks up the receiver and greets her next caller. "Hello, Amber," says the well-spoken gentleman. "My name is Jonathan Garner, store manager of Green's Electrics in the city centre. My staff and I are regular listeners to your show and are interested in your investigation into the whereabouts of the band Hell Freeze."

"Thank you, Mr Garner," beams Amber. "I'm glad you're all enjoying my show. Do you have any information for me?"

"I do indeed," says Jon. "Angel Mancini, the lead singer, was in our store just yesterday."

"Well, that's good, isn't it?" asks Amber. "He must be doing OK, possibly happily retired, if he is in your store buying things from you? I know he was the only one out of all the bandmates who was still working in showbiz after the band broke up."

"Actually," continues Jon, "he wasn't buying anything. In fact, he looked in dire need of a bath and a good meal. He is sleeping rough and he is always hanging around the shops near my premises. He only came into my store to watch the Liz McLarnon interview and my assistant, Eva, recognised him. When you approach him, he will pretend he doesn't speak English too well. The man obviously has his pride."

"That's tragic," cries Amber. "Mr Garner, would you mind if I call into your shop and you can point him out to me? With the help of the radio station, I can get him off the streets."

"Please do, Amber," says Jon. "If there is anything I can do from my end, please do not hesitate to ask."

Amber's studio phone is red-hot as the calls continue to flood in about the Hell Freeze members. "Angel rescued me from a gang," "Moose trains with me and can move trucks with his bare hands," "Liz is my boss," "Ronnie does my garden for me."

Although some of the calls and claims are totally unbelievable, Amber feels she can look into most of the listeners' observations. Nevertheless, she now has enough concrete information to go on to forge ahead with her investigation.

Amber's first point of contact would be Carl Martinez. She would go to Candy's to see him tomorrow before her show and try to secure an interview with him. That was the plan!

Amber wraps up her show and puts the recording on for the commercial break for the presenter taking over for DriveTime. Just then, her producer, Jack, pops his head around the door. "You're wanted in the managers' office, Amber," he tells her. This usually meant you were being disciplined. What had she done wrong? She felt so good on-air and the majority of the listeners now seem to like her.

Were her ratings down? Had there been that many complaints regarding her show?

Amber raps the managers' office door nervously. "Come in," says programme controller Gary Bryson, cheerily. At least he is in a good mood.

"Aaaahhh, there she is," smiles Gary. "How are you, sweetheart? Can I get you a coffee or anything to drink?"

"I'm fine, thank you, Gary, and coffee would be lovely," replies Amber. She did not expect this at all!

"Amber, I've brought you in because I want to personally commend you on your show," enthuses Gary. "Everyone is raving about it and your idea for tracing the members of Hell Freeze. That is a very original, but very daring, idea! Myself and the rest of the management team are absolutely delighted."

"Thank you so much, Gary," replies Amber. "That really means a lot."

"How far along are you so far?" asks Gary.

"I've not actually started it yet," Amber informs him. "I am planning to go to Carl Martinez's book signing at Candy's Book Store tomorrow morning before my show. I will, hopefully, be able to get an interview with him for the station. I also have information on the Mancini brothers and Liz McLarnon so I'll keep working through it over the course of the weekend and early next week."

"That really is amazing, Amber," says Gary. "It sounds like you have it all planned out. Please keep us posted on how you are getting on."

"Don't worry, I will," beams Amber. "Thank you so much again."

She now has approval from senior management.
There is definitely no turning back.

Chapter 4:
The Ball Starts Rolling

It is early on a Friday morning and Amber has barely slept all night. She is super excited about what lies ahead for her today and she was afraid she would over-sleep and miss Carl Martinez's book signing. She really hoped that Carl would be able to take time out of his busy schedule to talk to her. Liz arrives early at Candy's Book Store. There is already a massive queue outside the store and security staff are only allowing so many people in at a time. She hears the excited chatter of the Hell Freeze fans waiting in the line. She even hears her own name mentioned as well as her radio show. Amber smiles with pride as it seems that she has helped contribute to the publicity of Carl's book signing.

Amber gets to the front of the queue where she is finally allowed into the store. Carl Martinez is sitting at a long table with his pop-up poster behind him advertising his newly published book. He has the same cheeky smile that she knows only too well from all her mother's photos and posters of the band. His once long, curly, dark hair is now cut short, slicked back and there are a few grays beginning to come through at the sides and he sports a trendy goatee beard. He wears a leather waist coat over his tee-shirt, a pair of comfortable jeans and biker-style boots. He still looks very much like your typical rock star of that era.

It is now Amber's turn to have her book signed. "Hello, Mr Martinez," she greets him showing her I.D card. "My name is Amber Groves from Golden Plus FM."

Carl's face lights up even more. "Amber," he smiles as he gets up and shakes her hand. "It's so good to put a face to a name and a voice! Please call me Carl, everyone does. Thank you so much for all the mentions on air. They have helped my book sales no end! I have been listening to your show and I am excited to hear about your investigation. How are you getting on with it?"

"You're this first member I have met in person so far, although I do have leads on three of your bandmates that I am planning to follow up when I finish my show this afternoon," Amber informs him. "Can I leave you my business card and we can chat later? I can see you're busy."

Amber can hear fans muttering impatiently behind her. Carl smiles as he accepts her card. "Thank you SO much for doing this, Amber. It is all very much appreciated and I will definitely be in touch. If I don't contact you today, I will contact you by lunchtime tomorrow tops. Aaww, I can't wait to tell my dad about this!"

"Goodness," Amber gasps. "Well, I'll let you get on. There are lots of people who really want to see you. Thank you so much, Carl. I'll look forward to catching up later."

"Definitely," exclaims Carl, giving her a double thumbs up and waving to her as she leaves him to pay for her signed book.

Amber has gotten off to a flying start. Drummer Carl Martinez from Hell Freeze is keen to chat to her and is eager to get reunited with his former bandmates. Now she has something solid to tell her listeners and management team when she goes on air at lunch time. Better still, Jose Martinez, the band's former manager is still alive. She could possibly get chatting with him too on what it was like to manage one of the most successful rock bands of all time.

After her show, Amber's next point of contact was Green's Electrics where she hoped store manager Jonathan Garner can give her a lead on what he had previously told her about Angel. She enters the store to see a middle-aged, business-like gentleman and a sales assistant in her forties talking shop behind the cash registers. She approaches the counter. "Hello," she greets them. "I was wondering if I could possibly speak to Jonathan Garner?"

The middle-aged gentleman smiles. "That's me. How can I help you, miss?"

Amber shows her I.D and introduces herself to the gentleman with the familiar voice. "I was wondering if you had seen Angel today, Mr Garner?"

"Good to meet you, Amber," replies Jon. "He should be out there right now. Please come with me."

Jon and Amber make their way to the exit. This is a very poor place and there are so many homeless people. They both scan the busy street.

"Look," whispers Jon. "Right over there. Eva and I are positive that man is Angel." He points at a long-haired, bearded man who is sitting on the pavement minding his own business as he reads a newspaper. Amber approaches him and crouches down so that she is at eye-level with him. There is no mistaking him. This is definitely Angel, her mother's all-time crush. He looks at her with his deep, warm, brown eyes from behind his scruffy get up.

"Sir, do you mind if we chat?" Amber asks him.

Angelo puts down his newspaper and, in his broken English, he asks: "How can I help you, miss?"

Amber shows her I.D and introduces herself. "It has come to my attention that you are no ordinary man," she smiles. "You are, in fact, rock God Angel Mancini."

That did it. His cover was blown! Angel gets up and bolts like a star sprinter as Amber chases behind him, trying her best to keep him in her sights. For an older man, Angel is still super fit! Amber chases Angel for what feels like forever. She couldn't let him escape or he would move on and she would need to start her search for him all over again. She watches as he makes a sharp turn and she follows him. Unfortunately for Angel, it is a dead end. They are both out of breath from all the running as they stand staring each other out for a few moments.

"Please, Angel," begs Amber as she tries to get her breath back. "I only want to help you."

"If you really want to help me you'll leave me alone," replies Angel, no longer speaking in his fake Italian accent. "I only want peace and I certainly DO NOT want anyone to see me like this."

"Angel, if that's what you really want then I respect your wishes but, first, please listen to what I have to say," says Amber.

Angel realises that the young presenter is not taking no for an answer. "OK," he sighs. "But, please, no pictures."

"I promise," Amber assures him. "As you can see, I am here on my own. Right, here is the low-down. I am currently running a project on my radio show all about your band, the whereabouts of your members and a possible reunion. I spoke to your drummer, Carl, this morning about possibly reuniting the band and he is very keen to see how you are all doing."

"Carl," says Angel with sadness in his voice. "He was my best friend and right hand man since we started middle school together right up until the band broke up. Unfortunately, we were a dreadful influence on each other towards the end which was why we ended up in the mess we were in. I saw he was doing the book signing this morning and good to see that so many people remember us. I would love to talk to Carl again but look at me. I was the lead singer, for crying out loud, now I am just a bum living on the streets with absolutely nothing to show for it. What a tremendous fall from grace. Thank God Carl seems to have cleaned himself up and got dry though."

"Bad fortune happens to us all at some point in our lives," says Amber. "Anyway, you must be clean and sober now too. Gosh, I struggled to keep up with you during that flipping chase!"

Angel chuckles at this.

"Let's, at least, get you cleaned up and somewhere to sleep," says Amber. "I am due a catch-up with Carl again either tonight or tomorrow. Come on, Angel. It will make you feel better."

Angel shakes his head. "I can't accept that," he says. "It's far too much."

"I work in radio," Amber assures him. "I have approval from senior management and a blank cheque. We can get you cleaned up and a place to stay before we meet up with Carl."

Angel laughs when he realises that Amber has answers for everything: "OK, you're on. Thanks."

"Amazing," cries Amber excitedly as she claps her hands. "Let's go."

Amber and Angel walk into the well-established beauty salon on the high street. The staff and customers all turn and look at the odd pair in disbelief. There is Amber, who could pass for a top young business woman, accompanied by a dishevelled, old man who looks as though he has not seen so much as a bar of soap in years. A member of staff approaches them. "Can I help you, miss," he asks.

"YES," replies Amber. "We'll take the whole package deal please. Give my friend the works!"

The beauty therapist grimaces as he looks at Angel with disgust. "We'll have to take the payment up front and a job like this will cost you extra," he informs Amber.

"DONE," she replies and turns her attention to Angel. "What size do you wear?" she asks him. Angel looks at her blankly.

"It's OK, I'll figure it out," she giggles as she skips out of the salon, leaving the therapists to do their job. "See you in a couple of hours. Be good and don't go anywhere."

Amber returns to the salon in just under two hours later and the male beauty therapist who had previously served her beams with pride as he welcomes her back. She scans the salon floor but Angel is nowhere to be seen. WHERE THE HELL IS HE?

"The dirty, cheating fucking old hobo," Amber curses angrily.

"You know, an educated girl like you should know that you shouldn't swear out loud like that," says a familiar voice. "It's bad for the soul as well as the environment and is scientifically proven to turn the air blue."

Amber turns her head, very slowly, to the source of the voice. There stands a tall, handsome gentleman with Latin looks and distinct warm, brown eyes. His long beard is now gone and he is clean-shaven. His once long, matted, salt and pepper hair is shaved in at the back and sides and neatly cut and styled at the top. The leather jacket, shirt and form-hugging black jeans that Amber had given the salon staff for him to change into fit him perfectly and he looks about twenty years younger than when she left him. NOW she realises why her mother loves him so much. Angel raises a hand to Amber and gives her a half smile. Amber shrieks with delight, runs up and down the salon floor and peaks out from behind two female members of staff. "OH MY GOD!" exclaims Amber. "You look like...A ROCK STAR!"

"Cheers," says Angel quietly.

"Come on," says Amber, taking Angel by the arm. "We need to find a good hotel!"

Meanwhile, all the salon staff and customers are all sniggering because that just DID NOT sound right. Angel looks over his shoulder at the salon staff and customers who are all having a great laugh at his expense. "Help me," he mouths.

"Well, that's much better," Amber smiles with delight. "Now, where did I park my car?"

"Sorry, Amber, do you mind if we walk?" asks Angel.

"Walk?" asks Amber, surprised. "Didn't you get enough exercise from today's run?"

"Put it this way," says Angel with a wry smile. "You should think yourself lucky that you'll never experience the pleasure of a back, sack and crack wax. Those bloody things sting like Hell and that therapist enjoyed it TOO much!"

"Sorry, Angel," says Amber as she laughs out loud. "Beauty is pain."

Amber is feeling pleased with herself that she has managed to track down two of the members from Hell Freeze and they are both up for the reunion. She can't wait to get back on air to tell her listeners and check in with management at work. Also, how does she tell her mother that she went back to a hotel room with the man she has swooned over since her teenage years?

Back at the hotel, Amber carries on with her investigation as she asks Angel various questions about his time with the band, his relationships with manager Papa Joe and the different members. Angel speaks about how he and his best friend Carl from middle school had the idea of forming a rock band as they were both passionate about music from a very young age. The duo had busked on the streets for several months in all weather conditions, Angel on his accoustic guitar as he sang and Carl on his drum kit.

The two friends later decided they needed some real eye candy for the girls so they recruited Angel's older brother Mario. He was a strong boy, two years older than Angel and Carl who had become known as Moose due to his obsession with the gym, boxing and other sports. With a lot of fighting along the way, Angel taught Moose a few chords on the electric guitar until he finally got the hang of it. Despite being a dreadful student, Moose picked up the guitar very well indeed and was now passable as a lead guitarist.

They now needed a bass player. Moose said he knew somebody from his year at university who could possibly do the job but he was hesitant to ask him. Ronnie Buchanan hailed from the Scottish Highlands and, although they were pleasant to each other in passing, he and Moose were like night and day. Moose was your typical jock who could turn his hand to any sport. He had the looks, the physique and he could get any girl he wanted. All he had to do was flex his biceps or flash his seriously toned abdominals. Ronnie, on the other hand, was the quiet, studious type. He was extremely clever and once the other three guys got to know him, they found he was hilarious and could always make light of a bad situation AND he liked his nights out, beer and motorbikes. At the audition, it came to light that Ronnie was also an excellent song writer and that he had a decent singing voice that harmonised really well with Angel's vocals. He was recruited as their bass player and backing vocalist.

Having lost their keyboard player, Wullie McLarnon, due to the onus of being a law student, finding a replacement to fill his massive shoes was a living Hell. The guys had seen numerous unqualified and unreliable disasters until one day, years later, Papa Joe arrived home with 15-year-old Liz McLarnon in tow having spotted her as one of the local schools were taking part in the recording of his radio station's Christmas jingle. Liz had been banished to the piano by her music teacher due to her exceptionally bad singing as she was "away off key and singing like a goat." From there, Papa Joe went home and pre-warned the now thirty-something rockers that their next potential keyboard player was a girl and to "keep an open mind." Young Liz smiled confidently as Papa Joe introduced the band mates one by one. When it came to her audition Angel, Moose and Ronnie were absolutely blown away.

"The job's yours, kid," Moose exclaimed excitedly in his deep, husky voice.

"Hang on, Moose," yelled Carl. "What gives you the right to...?"

"Come on, Carl," Moose shouted back, now standing over him in an intimidating manner. "We've not seen anyone with this much technical knowledge or skill level since Wullie! We NEED a good keyboard player for this gig, which is in just three weeks, maybe even permanently. She's a raw talent and we are NEVER going to find anyone else this good!"

As a Scottish girl living in the States, Liz could not hide her amusement at the sound of an American man attempting to say a Glaswegian man's name.

Following the death of his mother, Wullie was 20 years old when he moved to the States with his father, three younger brothers and then six-year-old Liz and he refused, point blank, to go with any other version of the name he had been known as ever since he could remember. He joined Hell Freeze having replied to an advertisement for a keyboard player that Angel and Carl had posted in the university where he was studying.

Liz chuckled to herself as the two bandmates continued their argument.

"I'm not afraid of you, you big chunk," Carl shot back. "Get away from me! I am talking from a business point of view. She is only a child and she will be a liability."

"I've got your big chunk," growled Moose. "I am talking from a business point of view too! She is a super talented child who will be working with six responsible adults. Sorry, make that FIVE responsible adults and YOU! By the way, a gentle reminder that it was your own father who brought Liz to audition in the first place so he obviously sees great potential in her too. His business and all that. Liz, I am so sorry about this..."

The two men were almost coming to blows when Liz interrupted them: "Moose, are you talking about Wullie McLarnon by any chance?"

"YES," exclaimed Angel. "Have you been following us that long?"

"I suppose I have," replied Liz. "Wullie is my brother. He taught me almost everything I know about the keyboard, the technical side of it and songwriting."

Wullie had come from a huge family which comprised of seven brothers and one baby sister. Liz must have been the "gifted" sister that he had often spoken so lovingly of, which explained why she wasn't phased when talking and performing in front of the four long-haired biker men who were all around twenty years her senior and ages with her four eldest brothers. "Liz was wise beyond her years, used to the company of older men and could speak their language for the most part, especially when it came to sports and motorbikes."

Liz later confessed that she had been more afraid of Ronnie's then girlfriend Debbie, who had greeted her with silence and a cold stare on answering the door to her and Papa Joe on arrival at the appartment. Debbie's tune soon changed during Liz's audition. As soon as Liz had finished playing her first track, Debbie bounced into the room with the brightest, most beautiful smile. The tall, blonde beauty looked like a supermodel of that era and that smile was her best feature.

"My goodness, baby girl," cried Debbie. "Was that you playing the keyboard?"

"Ah, our Debbie," Moose smiled warmly as he sat back in his seat. "The voice of reason."

"Guys, we HAVE to have her," exclaimed Debbie, hugging Liz from behind.

Angel, Moose and Ronnie all agreed while Carl scowled, not daring to argue with Debbie! So it was agreed, young Liz was to become their new keyboard player.

"Amber," says Angel, nervously, as he snaps back to reality. "I've did a real dreadful thing."

"What?" Amber asks, surprised. Just then, her phone rings. "Sorry, Angel, I need to take this."

The call is from a unknown number. "Hello, Amber," says a familiar voice on the other end. "It's Carl Martinez. How did you get on?"

"Carl, it's so good to hear from you," exclaims Amber, who now has the phone on loudspeaker so that Angel can hear. "I got on great. I am at Rushmount Hotel with Angel right now."

"Wow, that was fast," says Carl excitedly. "I'll be there in ten."

In what felt like no time at all, Carl arrives. He greets Amber and as soon as he sees Angel, he shakes his hand and pulls him into a tight hug. It is an emotional time as the two one-time best friends are reunited with each other. Amber leaves quietly, allowing the two men to catch up, as she plans to continue her quest.

Chapter 5:
Amber's First Challenge

With the reunion of the band members well under way, Amber carries on with the intention of tracking down the other two that she has leads for. This next part could very well be awkward as Amber understands that Moose and Liz had not parted amicably. She approaches Trojans' Fitness Gym and she feels a pang of guilt as she has not made use of her membership at all this year. Working behind reception is a burly, latino man who looks to be in his fifties. "Good evening," he greets her with a dazzling, bright white smile.

"Hello," says Amber. "Are you Mr Breitner?"

"That I am not," smiles the man. "I am Marco Pieraccini, co-owner of this fine establishment. Lukas is out of office for today. Is there anything I can help you with?"

"I hope so," replies Amber as she shows Marco her I.D. "My Name is Amber Groves from Golden Plus FM and I am looking for Mario Mancini. I understand that he works here?"

"He does indeed, Miss Groves," says Marco, excitedly. "Lukas told me to expect you. That is a very exciting project you are working on. Moose, or Mario as he prefers these days, is off duty now and is having a workout of his own. I will show you where he is. Please come with me."

Marco leads Amber to a large, mirrored studio that is wall-to-wall with heavy gym equipment. "Look," smiles Marco, pointing in the direction of the smiths machines. "That beauty right over there."

"Oh my God," Amber gasps in shock. The years have not been kind to Moose at all. He looks very old and frail now. He is hunched over an inclined bench as he struggles to curl a three-kilogram dumbbell and he looks to be about ninety pounds soaking wet. Marco bursts out laughing when he realises who Amber is looking at.

"No, no, no," laughs Marco. "THAT one. The one in the white tank."

"WOW!! This is more like it," whispers Amber excitedly. If anything, Moose has improved with age. His once long, dark, curly hair is now salt and pepper and cut short and he sports a trendy, neatly shaped, grey beard. His toned back and arms ripple with muscle under the lights and his bright white tank emphasises his tanned skin. It is also obvious that he is not one to skip leg day! Moose, who must now be about sixty years old, looks very youthful and obviously has no intentions of letting himself get old any time soon.

"Well, I'll leave you to it," smiles Marco. "Good luck and please keep us posted."

"Mr Mancini?" Amber asks.

Moose puts down his heavy dumbbells and looks at her. He has the same warm, deep, brown eyes as his brother. "I am Amber Groves from Golden Plus FM," she informs him, showing her I.D. "I am currently working on a project based on your band

and wondered if you would be interested in a reunion with your former bandmates? Many of my listeners are massive fans of your band and your work and are keen to hear about where you all are."

"No thanks," replies Moose, flatly.

"Please, at least listen to what I have to say," pleads Amber.

"Look, kid," replies Moose in his deep, gravelly voice. "I left the band twenty years ago, have never looked back and don't ever intend to. This is what I do now. If you are interested in personal training, however, I will happily see you for a free consultation. Other than that, please don't waste your time."

"Can I ask why you are so against it?" Amber presses. "Is it because of Liz? Aren't you curious about the welfare of your other band mates and what about your brother?"

"Like I have already said," continues Moose. "I am finished with showbiz. A good showman knows when to leave the stage and let younger blood take over. I had a good run which was great while it lasted but it's over now. As for my former bandmates they are all intelligent, talented people and I am sure they are doing just fine."

"Actually," replies Amber. "Angel has lost his fortune and is homeless. He has been for many years now."

"SHIT!" cries Moose. "Is he alright? Bloody Hell, how did this happen? He had so much going for him!"

For a man who wasn't supposed to show any emotion, Moose is tearing up. "It's OK," assures Amber. "He is in a safe place with your drummer Carl and they are both clean and sober. I can take you to them. Also, what about your ex-girlfriend Liz?"

"OK," says Moose. "I'll come and see the guys, thank you, but please just don't go there."

Amber doesn't reply as she realises she has touched a raw nerve. Moose has still not moved on from his break-up with Liz after all this time. He quickly cleans himself up, throws on a pair of jeans and a tee shirt and leads Amber to his black Mercedes. Mr Breitner was right when he said Moose lives in the gym. This magnificent car looks like it cost him a small fortune.

When they arrive at the hotel room, they are greeted at the door by Carl who is overjoyed to be reunited with another of his old friends. Carl high fives Moose and he returns the greeting with a few playful biffs before being led to the sitting room where Angel is waiting nervously. Angel is unable to contain his emotions as his older brother pulls him up by the hand and into a long, tight hug. Even Moose struggles to keep it together and Amber finds herself crying. She leads Carl out into the hallway, still with tears in her eyes.

"I have one more lead," Amber sobs. "I'll be back soon."

Carl brushes a tear from Amber's cheek and hugs her. "Thank you so much," he says quietly, fighting back his own tears. "For everything."

Following a tip-off from Liz McLarnon's business partner, Amber makes her way to Bikers' Nightclub where she hopes to get some information on Liz and how she could chat to her. Amber approaches a six-foot-plus, long-haired, leather-clad steward who is staffing the doors. He is a rough-looking character who definitely fits the theme of the rock-based night club.

"Aaaaahhhhh," smiles the steward. "You are the young lady leading this investigation into Liz's band. Exciting times indeed! You're in luck. Liz is working behind the bar tonight due to staff shortage. Please come in. Good luck and thank you."

Amber is amazed at the interior of Liz's impressive club. Aimed at rock and heavy metal fanatics, the decor is dark, metallic and there are displays of instruments the band members had played, various awards the band had won during their hay day, Hells Angels memorabilia as well as classic Harley Davidson motorcycles. Amber also notices the photos on the walls from when the band were touring worldwide, often rubbing shoulders with major celebrities of that era. Right now a young up-coming rock band is providing the music and setting the atmosphere and the tone of the club. The clientele is an older crowd of people, all dressed in their biker gear with the occasional woman sporting a very short dress or a cat suit. Still, the atmosphere is friendly and welcoming.

Amber approaches the bar and, sure enough, a tiny blonde woman also in biker gear is working behind the bar along with her other staff. Liz doesn't even look as though she stands as tall as five feet as she chats happily to her customers and larks around with her staff. Amber catches the attention of another member of bar staff and asks if Liz is on the premises tonight. The small, dark-skinned Glasgow woman smiles as she recognises Amber's voice.

"She is indeed," replies the lady. "I am Angie Hutton, Liz's business partner. It was myself who called you, Miss Groves. Thelma! There's somebody here to speak to you."

"Righto, Louise, ta," the small, blonde woman replies cheerily as she strides over.

"You must be Amber," says Liz in her broad Glaswegian accent as she looks up at Amber and gives her a firm handshake. Amber finds this comical as the deep voice just does not fit her tiny body. "I'm Liz. I have been following your investigation and it all sounds very exciting. Let's go through to the back office and chat."

"Thelma?" asks Amber, confused.

"It's a reference to the old Geena Davis and Susan Sarandon movie, 'Thelma And Louise'," Liz laughs. "Angie is not just my business partner but my partner in crime and she often accompanies me on my trips back home to Scotland. The poor soul moved over here with me after my graduation to start our business fourteen years ago and has been my rock ever since."

Goodness! This is indeed Liz McLarnon, Amber's first ever girl crush. She has to be around forty years old now although to look at her, her small stature, slight build and clear skin made it very difficult to tell her age. She and her business partner Angie look like teenaged girls from a distance. Anyway she looks happy and relaxed and, unlike her ex-partner Moose, she is excited to hear about Amber's investigation.

"Thank you so much for coming in," says Liz, handing Amber a bottle of water and laying out a selection of fruit and snacks. "How are you getting on with everything so far?"

"Well," replies Amber. "I have found three of your band mates so far: Carl, Angel and Mario. I have literally just left them at Rushmount Hotel."

"That's amazing," beams Liz. "How are they all doing?"

"Carl was the first one of the guys I met," Amber tells her. "A cheery, friendly man. From what I can gather, he's not working at the moment as he is caring for his father."

"Papa Joe is still alive?" cries Liz excitedly. "Oh, I'm sorry. I didn't mean that in a bad..."

"It's OK," Amber laughs. "Joe is fine. He is frail having survived cancer but is still fighting and very much with it as far as I can gather."

"That sounds like Papa Joe," smiles Liz. "What about my Moose? We didn't part on good terms at all but I never forgot him. Not a day has gone by when I've not thought about him. Is he alright?"

Amber sighs. "He is emotional," she says. "He has been the hardest nut to crack and he won't even let me use his stage name but he was anxious to see his brother."

"Emotional?" asks Liz, surprised. "He must be mellowing out in his old age. He very rarely or never shows his sensitive side. Obviously, things were very different when we were together but he always was the tough outer shell of the band. You say he was anxious to see Angel. Is he alright?"

"Angel is OK, all things considered," Amber tells Liz. "When I met him today, he said he had been sleeping rough for a number of years."

"NO," exclaims Liz. "He was all over the media doing all sorts of wonderful things at one point. He looked so clean and super fit. I was under the impression he had cleaned himself up and sorted himself out. What on earth happened?"

"I don't know...," Amber tails off as she remembers that Angel was going to tell her about a "dreadful thing" he had done. Was he in trouble with the law and on the run? She supposes that would be something that would come out in the wash now that he was being reunited with real friends and family. Amber looks at Liz, who is now in tears.

"He is certainly clean and sober now," Amber says positively. "He just needs somewhere permanent to stay."

"I'm glad he has managed to clean himself up," says Liz. "He was in a real bad way when I left him at the hospital all those years ago and I almost lost him. I can take him in. After all, he did it for me. For him to sleep rough for all that time without reaching out to anyone is just beyond criminal. He would always be the first to put his own hand out to help anyone who needed it. I'll be giving him a damn good talking to when I see him!"

"Please be gentle then," says Amber. "This has been a very emotionally tiring day for all of us and we have all cried heaps. Anyway, shall we go and join the party now?" Liz nods and smiles, wiping away her tears.

On arrival at the hotel room, the three former rock stars are chatting and laughing as though they have never been away from each other. The room falls silent as Amber walks in with Liz in tow. Carl's face lights up and he jumps up and hurries over to greet Liz.

"There she is," exclaims Carl as he high fives her, picks her up and whirls her round. "It's so good to see you, gorgeous. You look fantastic!"

"Thanks so much, Carl. As do you," she replies as she embraces him.

Liz looks at the two brothers. Angel is smiling, although he looks very nervous, and Moose is stoney-faced as though he would now rather be elsewhere.

"Angel," Liz cries excitedly as she rushes over and gives him a kiss and a hug. "How are you, big bro? It's so good to see you, my darling! You're looking well."

Angel looks over Liz's shoulder at Amber as though looking for guidance on what to do next. Amber smiles and nods at him.

"Um, good to see you too, little sis," replies Angel as he hugs her back. "I've missed you. Anyway, I'd best let you go and see Moose. I'm sure he's dying to talk to you, right Moose?" Angel gives his brother the side-eye because he knows he will play hard-to-get.

"How are you, Moose?" asks Liz as she takes both of her former lover's hands. She didn't expect him to be jumping for joy at seeing her but this was beyond awkward. He still hasn't forgiven her after all these years.

"Yeah I suppose I am OK, considering...," Moose replies flatly as he pulls his hands from Liz's.

"Moose, I really am sorry," says Liz. "For everything."

"It's OK," replies Moose even though Liz knows that things are far from OK as he can still barely look at her. "Look, it's getting late and I have a class early tomorrow morning. I need to go."

"Fine," says Liz. "Please, at least, come to mine for dinner tomorrow. We really need to sort things out. We are both adults and we can't leave it like this."

"We'll be there," interrupts Carl. "What's your address?"

"It's my dad's old place," replies Liz. "I'm sure you remember it, Carl. Please bring your dad."

Carl thinks back to the numerous times he had slept at Liz's childhood home when he was too tired to drive back to the bandmates' apartment after long days and nights of rehearsals having dropped Liz home. Either Liz's father or one of her brothers would insist that the guys or Debbie stay overnight if they were concerned for their safety. It was then that Liz had made the decision to move in with her bandmates. Anyway, it saved a lot of time when she had to fit her studies in too.

"Oh my God, your dad," gasps Carls as he realises he has not yet heard Liz mention her father.

"Dad's fine and I'm planning to bring him tomorrow," Liz assures him. "He wanted to downsize because all my brothers have moved away now. I bought the house from dad, bought him a bungalo and I employ my brother John as his carer."

"Amazing," Carl smiles with relief. "We'll look forward to seeing Big Tam tomorrow too then."

"Are you coming, Angel?" interrupts Moose.

"He's staying at mine," replies Liz as she gently

puts an arm around Angel's shoulders.

"Cool, cheers," Moose says to Liz, flatly, as he bids Angel and Amber goodnight and walks out the door. Carl takes Liz by the hand. "Don't worry, babe," he assures her. "I'll talk to him and make sure he's there tomorrow, even if I need to drag him myself!"

"Thanks, Carl," smiles Liz as she kisses him on the cheek. "I owe you one. See you tomorrow, darling."

"I'll need to get going too," says Amber although she looks concerned. "Will you be OK here, Liz?"

"I'll be fine, love," replies Liz. "Will you please join us for dinner tomorrow too? I really can't thank you enough for all you've done for us. We can maybe do a recording of the interview for your show?"

"It's mutual," smiles Amber. "You and the guys are helping me more than you know and, yes, I would love to come to you for dinner."

"Here is my address," says Liz, handing Amber a card. "See you tomorrow around six."

Liz turns her attention to Angel, her expression very different now. "As for you," she says angrily in her deep voice and thick Glaswegian accent that she knows Angel can understand fine. "I am majorly pissed off at you."

"Well that's milder than I expected," says Angel, looking down at the floor as tears start streaming down his face and drop onto the white, marble tiles.

"Angel! Why didn't you come to me?" asks Liz.

"I'm so sorry for everything, baby," replies Angel as he tries to steady his voice. "I never got the chance to apologise to you. I must have really hurt you and I have had nightmares about it ever since. The night of the last gig..."

"Angel, you blacked out backstage and never woke up," Liz interrupts. "You were not a well boy and I was surprised you and Carl even got through that gig. At least Carl had Papa Joe and all those medical professionals to take care of him. You only had naive little me. Moose couldn't even be with you because he had already promised to take Ronnie to the hospital to be with Debbie and their new baby who were both seriously ill. I took you to hospital later on because you were barely breathing. You could have died and it would have been my fault. Believe me when I tell you you're not the only one who has nightmares about that night. The difference is that mine are very real because I was sober!"

Liz is in tears, yet again, as she remembers how she had held Angel's hand, begging him to hold on and fight for his life.

"That was all that happened?" asks Angel, surprised.

"That was all that happened?" cries Liz. "I have no idea what you think happened, Angel. The truth is that I made the mistake of taking you home when I should have taken you straight to hospital after the gig. Maybe you woke up for a brief moment when we were at the house, continued to have a bad trip and now the demons are following you? Then I find out from that young girl that you have been sleeping rough when I could have given you a place to stay and helped you get clean. If I hadn't been home, my dad or any of my brothers would have been. They all know how good you were to me the whole time I was in the band. I dread to think how you got clean."

Angel laughs through his tears. "The good old cold turkey works a treat," he says.

"It's not funny, Angel," scolds Liz. "As a medic, I saw many people die when they tried coming off hard drugs like that and it would have been worse for you as you were homeless. Let's say you did what the demons are saying you did. Do you, honestly, think my dad and my eight brothers would have let you away with it? I was and still am their princess, for God's sake. They would have tracked you down and ended you. When I left you at the hospital, I left you two envelopes: one was your pay cheque from Papa Joe and the other one was a letter from me. If you had read that letter, you would have got the truth instead of that ugly imaginary scenario you got from the demons from your bad trip."

Angel still can't look at Liz. "I couldn't even bring myself to open that envelope," he told her as he continues to cry.

Liz puts a hand on Angel's cheek and turns his face to hers. "Angel, you DO NOT have that kind of badness in you," she reassures him. "You don't have a single bad blood cell in your entire body and I know you certainly would never have intentionally hurt me. The fact that you have punished yourself all this time says it all. Please believe me. You are innocent, I have no reason to distrust you and you need to stop beating yourself up for something you didn't even do. Now please let me help you."

"Are you telling me the truth?" asks Angel, this time looking Liz straight in the eye.

"Angel, a heinous act like that would be inexcusable

no matter how much I love you," cries Liz. "Alright, I am now speaking to you in my serious doctor voice and asking you this question as a medic. You don't need to answer me. I just want you to think about it. If this doesn't convince you, I have no idea what will. When you are as intoxicated as you were on the night of that gig, how reliable is your equipment?"

Liz raises her eyebrows. Angel laughs and blushes as he remembers how he had learned the hard way that if he wanted that kind of action and to get said equipment to work after a gig so he could live up to his reputation as a rock God, he couldn't drink at all.

"There's your answer," says Liz, calmly, as she hugs Angel tight and kisses him on the cheek. "Please come home, Angel. If you owe anyone anything, it's yourself. I've missed you, big bro."

"I've missed you too, little sis," replies Angel quietly as he hugs her back and accepts her invitation and, finally, the truth.

Meanwhile, you can cut the atmosphere with a knife inside Moose's black Mercedes. Apart from the very slight sound of the car engine, it is deathly silent.

"She's sorry, bro," says Carl as he breaks the silence. "She's genuinely sorry. What more do you want, in the name of God? Blood?"

"Not your business, Carl," warns Moose. "Tread very carefully."

"I'm not afraid of you, you old battleaxe," laughs Carl.

"I've got your old battleaxe," Moose glares.

"Seriously though," continues Carl. "You could have at least made the effort and spoken to her. She made the effort to come and see you and it is obvious she still cares for you AND she's single."

"Bull shit," scoffs Moose.

"OK," says Carl. "Maybe tonight wasn't the best set-up for you both. Maybe you need some alone time. Why don't you ask her to dinner, take her for a long drive, a walk in the countryside or something?"

"Hang on," laughs Moose. "You're giving me relationship advice?"

"Look, I know I'm not the best advert," says Carl. "I just know a good thing when I see it. You guys were great together. She loved you then and she obviously still does. She left all those years ago because she had to sort herself out. I don't know if you noticed, bro, but she was in a very bad way towards the end. We all were. I just don't want you to miss your chance. If you really want to save your relationship and try again, you'd better make your move soon before somebody else does. If you don't do it for yourself, do it for that young girl who has gone to the trouble of bringing us together. Please think about what I said."

They pull up outside Carl's apartment block. "See you tomorrow at 5.30 p.m sharp," Moose says with a warm smile. "Please make sure Papa Joe is ready."

"That's my boy," laughs Carl as they fist punch each other. "See you tomorrow and remember your mouthwash and your clean underwear!"

"Get out of here," laughs Moose as he begins to relax. "See you tomorrow, pal."

Meanwhile, Amber bounces through the front door of her parents' house to find that they are anxiously waiting up for her.

"Sorry I'm late," Amber apologises. "I am working on a massive project at work and didn't want to say anything in case it all fell through."

"We've been worried sick, darling," says Mrs Groves. "Where have you been?"

"Mom and Dad, you'd better sit down so I can tell you this," says Amber excitedly. "Like I said, it's a huge project and I have struggled to keep it to myself all week. My listeners have requested that I reunite the band Hell Freeze. Remember you were both massive fans back in the day?"

"That's awesome, honey," exclaims Mr Groves. "That is an amazing project indeed! How are you getting on with it all so far?"

"Dad, it has snowballed," beams Amber. "So far I have tracked down Carl, Angel, Moose and Liz."

"Aaww, my darling Angel," sighs Mrs Groves as she blushes, much to the annoyance of Mr Groves. "I hope I can get to meet him."

"Let's just calm down, Jenna," glares Mr Groves. "I still want a sparring match with that Moose character. I bet I could wipe the floor with him now!"

"You're still my number one, Matt," says Mrs Groves as she smiles at her husband.

"Please don't bother, Dad," laughs Amber. "Moose is in better shape than most guys my age AND I love you. Mom, I will get that arranged for you too. Anyway, I am tired after all my running around and crying today. Good night, Mom and Dad."

"Night, superstar," beams Mr Groves.

Chapter 6:
The Final Missing Piece

ngel wakes up with the sun shining into his room through the blinds. He looks at the alarm clock on the bedside table. 9.15 a.m. That was the longest, undisturbed sleep he had had since he and his bandmates had shared their mansion all those years ago. He didn't even have the nightmare that has plagued him since the night of the band's last gig of the farewell tour. Angel is finally at peace. He lies on his back under the bright, white duvet of his huge queen-sized bed and looks at the ceiling as he reflects on how different his life is at this very moment compared to when he left that hotel room to aimlessly walk the streets just yesterday morning. He is now reunited with his best friend, his brother and the woman he had always thought of as a little sister that he thought he would never be able to speak to again. She had even taken him in to live in her home, having reassured him that he had done no wrong. Life is finally good again.

Angel gets up and gets into the en-suite shower. He is cleaning himself up when he happens to look down. "Shit," he thinks to himself. "Where is my necklace?"

He looks, frantically, on the floor and in his bed. Nothing. Come to think of it, he hadn't remembered seeing it in the salon either. It may have fallen off during one of his many street fights or during his chase with Amber. It could be anywhere and he would never get it back now.

"Fuck," Angel says out loud as he sits down heavily on the bed, cupping his face in his hands. He has lost his most valued possession.

Meanwhile the warm-hearted, Scottish street sweeper is going about his work as usual. He whistles happily to himself as he enjoys the spring sunshine. Suddenly, he is interrupted by the wail of sirens and a speeding paramedics vehicle with flashing, blue lights. "Nothing too serious, I hope," he thinks to himself as he carries on working.

A little while later, the street sweeper rounds the corner to see the paramedics are loading a dead body into the back of their vehicle before driving off. Meanwhile, other homeless people are looking on with their heads bowed in prayer as they mourn the loss of another aquaintance.

"May God rest their soul," says the street sweeper as he looks down to pray. As he does so, something shiny catches his eye. He picks it up and examines it. It is an expensive-looking, distinctive, gold guitar pendant, still with the thick belcher chain attached to it. Why, he would recognise it anywhere. He reminisces about the time the owner had come into possession of it.

Ronnie Buchanan was enjoying a night in with his bandmates, his wife Debbie and manager Papa Joe as they celebrated their friend and bandmate Angel's 34th birthday. It was a bit of a non-event as it was a school night and all the band members still had their regular jobs and school to go to in the morning. They were all enjoying drink, food and music when 16-year-old keyboard player Liz came home, very late, from school. On approval from her father, she had recently moved into the band's tiny three-bedroomed apartment so that she could concentrate on rehearsals as well as her studies. She handed Angel a small, gift-wrapped box and kissed him as she wished him happy birthday. Inside the box was this custom-made guitar pendant that Angel had treasured, worn from then on and had never taken off. It was a cherished gift from a girl that he had grown very close to and loved like a little sister.

Ronnie snaps back to the awful reality. "Oh, God, please naw," he begs as he clutches the pendant. He now knows the truth about the homeless stranger he has often left food for and he is now gone forever.

"ANGEL!" shouts Ronnie as he breaks down and falls to his knees. He somehow summons the strength to get back up in order to search in vain for his friend who had become more like a brother to him back in the day. He passes a group of five other homeless guys.

"Hey, buddy," one of the men calls out. "Are you looking for Old Angelo?"

"Angelo?" asks Ronnie, with tears in his eyes. "Yes, I am. Have you seen him?"

All five of the guys are laughing. "He got chased up the high street by a fit, young hottie yesterday, my man," chimes in another one. "He's not been seen since. They're probably getting it on in a hotel room somewhere, the old fox. Some guys get all the luck."

Ronnie has a bad feeling and his stomach is in knots as he goes to look for his supervisor. He finally sees him. "Bloody Hell, Ronnie," says the supervisor. "It's not like you to cry. What's wrong?"

"I need to go home," Ronnie tells him. "I've just had news of a bereavement. It's my brother."

"So sorry, Ronnie," sympathises the supervisor. "Please get yourself away and take care, my good man, and let us know if we can do anything for you from our end."

"Thanks for understanding," replies a distraught Ronnie as he makes his way home to break the dreadful news to his wife and daughter.

Presently, Liz arrives home with her dad. The aroma of all the different flavours hits them as soon as they open the door. Angel has been busy as he is laying different types of food from meat joints, breads, salads, vegetables and desserts onto the long dining table that he has moved into the living room. His face lights when he sees Liz's dad. Standing at 6 ft 4 and now in his eighties, Big Tam McLarnon still has that air of authority about him. His salt and pepper curly hair is now bright white but he still has that distinctive smile with the piercing blue eyes.

"TAM," cries Angel as he strides over to greet his former manager. "It's so good to see you. How are you doing?"

"Hello, my son," smiles Tam as he embraces Angel. "Liz told me you had moved in. It's great to have you around again."

"Cheers, Tam," replies Angel. "Your daughter is an amazing woman."

"She is that," beams Tam. "I am so proud of my girl. By the way, your spread looks and smells fantastic."

Angel turns to Liz and smiles. "I hope you don't mind, Liz, I started early because I was bored. How anyone can watch that daytime crap on TV is beyond me."

"Not at all," replies Liz, happily. "You did a better job than I ever could. Thank you. You've definitely not lost your touch."

"It's the Italian in me," laughs Angel. "Works every time!"

Shortly afterwards, Amber arrives. "WOW, this is amazing," enthuses Amber as she looks at all the magnificent decor and paintings in the huge hallway of Liz's mansion. "Something smells delicious too."

"Thanks so much for coming, Amber," smiles Liz. "Angel was home alone today and he has been busy. Typical Italian boy. Please come and meet my dad. He helped Papa Joe manage us when we hit the big time."

Liz hands Amber a glass of champagne and leads her into the livingroom where she makes herself comfortable on a large, white leather sofa and chats with Angel and Tam while she waits for the rest of the bandmates to arrive.

The four are chatting and having a great laugh about old times when Moose arrives with Carl and Papa Joe.

"Hello, my baby girl," Papa Joe says with delight as he reunites with Liz. "It's so good to see you. There's no mistaking you. You are as stunning as ever."

"Thank you for coming, Joe," replies Liz. "It's been

far too long and we have so much catching up to do. My dad is here too. He is looking forward to seeing his old partner in crime again."

Carl high-fives Liz and hugs her in his usually cheery manner before he takes Papa Joe's arm and guides him into the living room where the two former managers greet each other with a handshake.

Liz turns her attention to Moose, who seems a lot more at ease than he was yesterday although still very quiet. "Thank you for coming along, Moose," she says as she hugs him. To her surprise, he hugs her back and holds her for a good few minutes.

"Moose?" says Liz nervously. "Are you free any time this week? I would like to take some time out to chat. Just us."

Moose gives her the warm smile that she remembers from their younger days. "Come to the gym tomorrow at 1 p.m," he says quietly. "I'm free then and will try to get my clients rescheduled for the day."

"I'll be there," smiles Liz as she puts her arm round his waist and guides him into the livingroom.

Everyone is chatting and enjoying the food and drink when the subject of Ronnie, the absent bass player, comes up.

"Actually, I know where Ronnie is," says Angel.

"Fuck sake, man, you know everything," laughs Carl.

"I hope for your sake that wasn't somebody else you let saunter past you as you slept on the streets," adds Moose. "For God's sake, bro. Why?"

Liz wraps her arms around Moose's broad shoulders. "We'll explain later, babe," Liz tells him quietly.

"Where is he then?" asks Carl.

Just then, the doorbell rings. Liz excuses herself to answer it. She opens the door to be met by the familiar figure of Ronnie who is dressed all in black and looks as though he has done a lifetime of crying. Behind Ronnie is Debbie who also appears very distraught and is being supported by a stunning young, blonde woman who looks like a very young Debbie.

"Ronnie and Debbie, it's so good to see you and you must be Caitlin," exclaims Liz as she greets the three of them.

"Liz, I hoped you would be here," Ronnie says through his tears. "I have dreadful news and there is no easy way to tell you. Angel is dead."

Debbie really breaks down at this and the young, blonde woman is also crying as she holds her mother to support her.

"No," replies Liz. "I've got Angel here along with my dad, Papa Joe, Moose and Carl. Please come in. We were literally just talking about you!"

Hearing the familiar voices, Angel comes into the hallway to see what's going on.

"Angel," cries Ronnie. "My God, pal, you gave me a Hell of a fright! Why did you not reach out? Surely to God you recognised me? You look fantastic and more like yourself now! I got this back for you." He hands Angel a small box.

Angel is delighted when he opens the box and sees his necklace. "Thanks so much, brother," he says, relieved. "I never thought I would see it again. Also, thanks for the sandwiches. At least I ate something most days."

"You could have had a bloody roof over your head and hot food instead of a stupid packet of cheap sandwiches," scolds Ronnie. "For God's sake!"

"It's OK, Ronnie," Liz says quietly. "I'll speak to you and Debbie privately later."

Moose and Carl come into the hallway to see what all the fuss is about and Ronnie and Debbie greet them.

"Guys," says Ronnie as he puts his arm around the shoulders of the young, blonde woman. "This is our Caitlin. She graduates from uni next year and will be following in her mum's footsteps."

"It's so good to finally meet you, Caitlin," smiles Liz. "Thanks for coming along. We will certainly be needing an extra pair of hands...that's if you're up for a job?"

"Thanks for having me, Auntie Liz," replies Caitlin. "Can I call you that? Sorry for gatecrashing your party. Mom and dad have told me so much about you and the guys and I would LOVE to come and work with you!"

"I am proud to be your Auntie Liz, sweetheart," says Liz as she hugs her. "You have become such a beautiful, well-mannered, intelligent young woman and you are doing your old folks proud."

Young Caitlin is almost star struck as she finally meets her father's four band mates that he and her mother have spoken so fondly of ever since she can remember. She didn't even need her parents to introduce them. Angel is the tall, handsome one who still has his good looks and is made to be the leading man, Moose is the fit, muscular one and

Carl is the small, cute, funny one with the dazzling, white smile and the sharp sense of humour.

Liz reports back to Amber. The old line-up is now complete with the five band members, the two managers and engineer are together again for the first time in twenty years and now they were ready for their interview.

Chapter 7:
The Interview

Eager to get to work, Debbie and Caitlin help Amber set up her recording equipment as the band prepares for their first radio interview in more than twenty years. They are now ready to go.

Amber: "Good afternoon. This is Amber at Golden Plus FM bringing to you the long-awaited interview with Hell Freeze, who are making their big comeback after twenty long years away from the spotlight. Guys, thank you for joining us. How does it feel to be back after all this time and how have you prepared?"

Moose: "I think we can all agree that it is nerve-wracking, to say the least. I mean, do our old fans remember us and how will we appeal to today's audience? As for the preparation, we all have loads of songs up here. The five of us have written songs for many years and it comes natural to all of us."

Everyone looks at Moose in pleasant disbelief. Of all the band members, he was the one who definitely did not want this reunion yet he was off to a flying start, answering the first question without even being prompted to do so.

Amber: "I am sure the question on everyone's lips is: 'What have you all been doing while you have been away?'"

One by one, the band talks about everything from solo careers, other careers in the music business, their professions away from showbiz, drug and alcohol addiction and the dark side of being in the spotlight and leaving the public eye.

Happy with her first major interview, Amber thanks the band and decides to wrap things up. Moose excuses himself and goes to get something from his car. He returns with two guitar cases, one of which he hands to Angel.

"Oh my God, bro," gasps Angel. "Where did you get this? I sold it many years ago because I was at the very end of my rope."

"I knew something had happened when I saw it for sale," Moose tells his brother. "I bought it at auction with the hope that I could return it to you one day. You'd BETTER make good use of it because I spent the last of my money on it!"

Liz gasps with delight as Angel opens the case to reveal the very guitar she had carried onto the tour bus on the night of their very last gig. "Unreal," she cries. "You see, everyone. There is a heart in there after all. A huge heart of gold at that!"

Moose playfully throws Liz over his shoulder as everyone laughs.

"OK," says Tam with a mischievous smile. "How about a wee jam for this young lady to treat her listeners to? Our Liz has her music room set up already."

"Agreed," exclaims Joe as he punches the air. "Are you young 'uns up for it?"

The bandmates, Debbie and Caitlin head through to Liz's spectacular music room and get organised. Amber is impressed by the set-up of the large room which consists of various magnificent musical instruments incuding a grand piano, various stringed instruments and guitars, a keyboard kit, a drum kit and various guitar amps. she watches and listens in awe as Angel and Ronnie sing note-perfect and the other band members play their instruments in harmony as though they have never missed a rehearsal. They play five of their biggest hit songs in order to make a good impression on the audience.

Amber is ecstatic. This interview had gone so much better than she had hoped. These guys are natural performers who have no problem speaking in front of an audience. Not only that, she also has a live recording to take back for her listeners. Tonight was a successful night indeed and Amber cannot wait to go on air and let her listeners hear the interview.

At the end of the performance Debbie, Caitlin and the bandmates help Amber pack up her equipment and take it to her van. Amber thanks everyone, one by one, for their support and participation. Just as she is heading to her van, she hears her name being called. It's Moose and he looks so much happier and relaxed then when she had first met him at the gym.

"Listen, Amber," he says. "I just want to apologise for the way I treated you the other day. It was all just so unexpected but I can't thank you enough for all your hard work. For everything."

"There is no need to apologise, Mario," assures Amber. "Lukas warned me that you might not be interested in a reunion and I really appreciate you coming along and playing with your band. You guys have definitely still got it!"

"Please, call me Moose," he replies. "After all, I'll need it for when we start performing again."

"Does that mean you've changed your mind?" asks Amber excitedly.

"We'll take it a day at a time," replies Moose. "We have today's young, sorry, younger blood to compete with and we still have a lot of work to do as a band. After all, we've not worked together for twenty years."

"This is amazing," Amber cries with delight. "Thank you so much, Moose. I'll look forward to following your progress. Oh, and what about Liz? Am I allowed to ask?"

"Again, baby steps," says Moose, very quietly, as he smiles warmly. "Thanks, Amber. Please drive safely and phone Liz as soon as you arrive home."

"Will do," smiles Amber. "See you soon, Moose, and thank you!"

Back indoors the management team, band members and engineers are talking excitedly about their band reforming and producing new material for the fans.

"Guys and gals," Liz interrupts the excitement with a serious business-like tone. "If we are all really serious about all of this, things will be VERY different to how we did it before. First of all, we will have more down time. When we were together before, we worked against the grind seven days a week and we barely stopped to take a breather. Even when we were sick, rehearsals and performances did not stop. Poor Ronnie and Debbie didn't even get a honeymoon after their wedding, for God's sake! We got so used to doing it that nobody noticed the strain we were all under and how ill it was making us mentally, emotionally and physically. There should be at least one day of the week when every single one of us puts our instruments and pens down and steps away. Also, we should have at least one annual holiday to completely relax and get away from it all. I don't know about you guys but I could never go through what we went through twenty years ago. We wore ourselves into the ground then so just think what it would be like now that we are older."

"Speak for yourself," laughs Moose. "In all seriousness though, you're right. We will definitely take things at a much slower pace this time and allow ourselves some well-needed time out."

Everyone is in agreement as they decide to start rehearsals again in the near future.

Meanwhile, Amber calls her boss from her van. "Hello?" says a sleepy voice at the other end of the phone.

"Hi, Gary, it's Amber," She sings excitedly.

"Oh, hi, Amber," yawns Gary. "What's up?"

Amber notices the time on her van clock: 2.20 a.m! "Oh I am so sorry, Gary," Amber apologises. "I didn't realise it was so late. I got so carried away with the excitement of everything and wanted to run some things past you before I go on air tomorrow."

"That sounds very exciting, Amber," enthuses Gary. "Please tell me what you have."

"I would be quicker telling you what I don't have," exclaims Amber. "I had the most beautiful dinner with Hell Freeze at Liz McLarnon's mansion tonight. The whole band, the management team and the band's engineers were all there. They gave me the most amazing interview, performed some of their hit songs and let me take pictures for the station website. I was planning to play the entire interview on air tomorrow during my show."

"Fantastic, my dear," cheers Gary. "You have done an amazing job and I'll look forward to tomorrow. Goodnight, Amber."

Chapter 8:
Amber's Recognition

Amber arrives at Golden Plus FM Head Quarters to a completely different atmosphere to what she is used to. Every presenter who works in the building seems to have turned out to congratulate her on her project and she is greeted at reception with balloons, party poppers, food, drink and lots of cheering from management, presenters and other staff. Following some chat and celebrations with her fellow staff members, Amber and Producer Jack head into the studio to commence their show where they would air what feels like a long-awaited interview with a band many of their listeners had been curious about for years.

"Good afternoon, ladies and gentlemen," Amber greets her audience. "You are listening to Lunchtime With Amber on Golden Plus FM. Thank you for joining us on this fine afternoon. As promised, I have an interview with the band Hell Freeze and a mini set from them to play for you. I plan to play the interview again several times during the week so please feel free to call or text which times suit you best. So many of you have requested this interview and I don't want you to miss it. I would like to say and extra special thank you to Derek and his team at Moonlight Laundry Services for their suggestion to trace the band members as well as to other listeners for your invaluable advice. Ladies and gentlemen, here it is. The interview you have been waiting for. Please sit back and enjoy."

Amber presses play and she and producer Jack are busy throughout the entire show taking calls from ecstatic listeners. Amber has finally earned the respect she had desired from all angles including her management team, fellow presenters who had once jeered at her and from her listeners. She is now finding her work very rewarding and she is feeling accomplished.

Chapter 9:
Moose and Liz

Liz arrives at Trojans' Fitness Gym to meet with Moose. She is feeling nervous as this is the first time she is going to be alone with him in twenty years. Liz is greeted on arrival by Lukas and Marco, who are delighted to see her again and excited at the prospect of Hell Freeze reforming. She smiles as she remembers both men as young gym instructors, now they own the gym.

Lukas and Marco had enjoyed successful athletic careers during their younger days. Lukas was a world champion body builder while Marco has several world titles under his belt from when he competed in several martial arts disciplines. He had even taken Liz under his wing when she was going through her "fat, ugly phase" when she was sixteen years old and struggling with the limelight as she was compared to her seemingly perfect counterparts. Liz worked hard, got herself in fantastic shape and achieved her Karate black belt. Even now, Marco claims that Liz was one of his best students of all time.

Moose finishes up with his personal training client and greets Liz with a kiss and a hug. "I'll be back in a couple of hours," he says as he winks at Lukas and Marco.

"Mario, my old friend," laughs Lukas. "You're owed time. Why don't you take a few days off and enjoy some down time with your beautiful lady and we'll see you on Thursday?"

"Go on, Mario," Marco chimes in. "At the rate you work, you should be able to afford a mansion, a Lamborghini and countless Harley Davidsons. I'll reschedule your clients for you."

"Thanks, guys," says Moose. "See you on Thursday."

Moose and Liz are enjoying a stroll through the park in the crisp, spring sunshine.

"Sorry I've not said much these past couple of days," says Moose. "What's been happening with you...for the past twenty years?"

"I'm sorry I made such a quick exit," says Liz with sadness in her voice. "None of the decisions I made were easy, even though I think back now and realise I did the right thing."

Moose hangs his head as he remembers the day he had proposed to Liz and how she had turned him down. The saving grace was that there were no witnesses even though walls have ears and people discover things easily.

"Moose," Liz breaks the silence. "I never stopped loving you. You were my first love AND my last. I had to get away from here, away from the paparazzi and away from everyone who knew me or I would never have lived to tell the tale. Anyway, I wanted to go to uni as I had already postponed that to dedicate all my time to the band."

"I don't understand," replies Moose. "You had everything going for you here. I hear you now have your solo career as well as your nightclub. You could have done that back then too and you could have continued your studies here."

"I don't know if any of you noticed," says Liz in a matter-of-fact tone. "I wasn't in a good place. I was suffering badly from stress, anxiety and anorexia. I was constantly worried about Carl and Angel as all I could do was watch them both slowly kill themselves with drugs, alcohol and over work. When Debbie became pregnant, we should all have been over-joyed for her and Ronnie but we all knew, deep down, that there was something not right with the pregnancy from day one. Then there was the constant grind of rehearsals, peformances and sleepless nights for all of us. How you managed to hold it together, I'll never know."

"Please believe me when I tell you I did my share of crying behind closed doors too," says Moose. "I felt helpless as I watched everyone suffer, including you. I am labelled as the tough guy of the band, yet I was powerless to do anything to help any of you. I come across as tough and insensitive but you have no idea how much I was hurting too."

"But you competely disappeared off the face of the Earth," replies Liz. "I was in Scotland for six years so I could under-go my treatment and, eventually, do my PhD."

"No way," exclaims Moose. "You're a doctor?"

"Uh-hu," smiles Liz. "I thought I would follow in my brother Harry's footsteps. He put me up and supported me through absolutely everything from my treatment, to my studies, to my new job. Unfortunately, the job wasn't what I thought it was going to be. My dream was to help as many people as possible but I found out, the hard way, that the medical profession doesn't always work like that. As a junior doctor I was constantly stressed, overworked, unable to help people I really wanted to help and I could feel myself relapsing. Not a good look for a doctor. Anyway I missed the U.S, my dad, all my friends and YOU. The first thing I did when I got back here was go to your mum's house to look for you."

Moose stops in his tracks. "Mom?" he asks, shocked.

"I know," says Liz, quietly. "You've not been to her house in twenty years and neither has Angel. I take her for lunch every Tuesday and she always, without fail, asks me if I have any news on her boys. The last time she heard of the slightest trace of your existence was when you put several thousand dollars into her bank account following our very last gig. She always tells me she would rather have had you and Angel home than any God's amount of money."

"Aw, Christ," says Moose, cupping his face in his hands. "Of all the people who did anything at all for my Mom, it had to be her son's ex-girlfriend. It's getting cold. How about we go back to mine for a hot drink?"

"Let's," smiles Liz as she takes Moose by the hand and leans her head against his shoulder.

Moose and Liz arrive at Moose's run-down fourstorey apartment block. His tiny, one-bedroomed apartment is on the top floor of the old building.

"Sorry about the apartment," Moose apologises. "As you can see, fitness instructors do this job for the out-come rather than the in-come."

"It's fine," assures Liz. "You always did keep your

place spotless. Anyway I'm here to see you, not the apartment. Sure, didn't we live in much more cramped conditions when I first moved in with you?"

"Yeah, I suppose we did," laughs Moose.

Moose and Liz laugh as they remember their old three-bedroomed apartment that they had shared with Papa Joe, Debbie and their bandmates. The front room, which was meant as the living room, doubled up as the band's recording studio. It was crammed with an old black leather three-piece suite, a television stand and all the band's musical instruments and amplifiers as well as Debbie's sound and recording equipment. On their very rare days off rehearsals, the band used this room for eating and chilling out as the kitchen was too small for a dining table. However when Debbie had recording and mixing to do, everyone would be banished from that room so that she could get her work done in peace.

Ronnie and Debbie shared the other front room which just accomodated their double bed and no more, Carl and Papa Joe shared the middle room and probably the one with the most space while Liz shared the last room with Moose and Angel. The guys had bunk beds and Liz slept in a small single bed next to theirs. Nobody minded the lack of space as long as they could do their rehearsals in peace. The biggest bug bear for everyone, however, was the fact that they only had one tiny bathroom among seven adults, which was no fun when everyone had work and school to get ready for in the mornings.

Liz thinks back to the night she and Moose first got together. By now, the rising stars were doing well and had long since given up their full time jobs to dedicate all their time to showbiz. Liz, herself, had declined her unconditional acceptance for medical school as she didn't want to let her bandmates down and leave them without a keyboard player at such a crucial stage in their career. The bandmates, Debbie and Papa Joe had moved into a respectable two-storey mansion that Liz had often stopped to admire as she walked home from school. It was like a palace and was a far cry from their previous residence. When she noticed it up for sale one day, she told Papa Joe and her bandmates about it and they snapped it up. Now everyone, apart from Ronnie and Debbie, had a bedroom each, the house consisted of two decent-sized bathrooms as well as the en-suites in Liz's room and in Ronnie and Debbie's. There was a conservatory that was converted to accomodate a hot tub, a steam room and a minibar.

It was a Saturday and Papa Joe was away for the weekend with managers and presenters from his radio station as they celebrated winning a major award. Debbie was also away for the weekend as she attended a girlfriend's hen party. Liz, now 19 years old, had plans for that night too. She had agreed to go on a dinner date with music producer Jason Hitchens, who was very well known and respected in the industry. That just left the four guys, three of whom had decided on a wild night out just because they could. Moose had been very solemn and unusually quiet all day and it had not gone unnoticed by the rest of his bandmates, who had tried in vain to get him to go on this wild night out. Moose being Moose would not budge, preferring to stay home and do a workout. It was then that the rest of the bandmates had realised that Moose had not been on any wild nights for almost a year now. Even when he did go out, there were no more all-nighters. He would always come home early with Ronnie, who was madly in love with Debbie and had no interest in other girls. Was Moose slowing down in his old age as he was nearing forty? Did he have a secret girlfriend? Nobody knew as he was never one to talk about either his feelings or his private life.

Hitchens arrived at 6.30 p.m in a silver chauffeur-driven Limo to collect Liz. She looked very elegant in a floor-length, sparkly white dress that was cut to show one shapely leg, white bolero jacket and silver stiletto heels. Everyone, except Moose, wished Liz luck on her date and said they would see her tomorrow. Moose said nothing and refused to look up as he continued to watch the live boxing match on TV.

Little did the guys know, Liz did not intend this meeting with Hitchens as a date but as a business meeting. Papa Joe and the band had recently had serious issues with their record label and they were on the verge of being dropped. Liz had gone on the date with the hopes of securing a much better deal for herself and her band mates.

Hitchens and Liz arrived at the classy restaurant and were seated by waiting staff. Hitchens had already ordered champaign on ice which was ready to serve at their table. The pair sipped champaign as they waited for their food. "Thank you for coming out on this fine evening, my dear," said Hitchens, his toothy smile not quite reaching his eyes.

"Thank you for the invite," smiled Liz, although she could feel that something was off.

"My pleasure," replied Hitchens. "I see you are a very beautiful, talented young woman with an abundance of great potential. I have a deal for you that could make you very comfortable for the rest of your life."

"Thank you," replied Liz. "That will be some well-needed exciting news for me to tell the guys when I get home. What will be expected of us and what kind of deal are you offering in return?"

"Liz, my dear," said Hitchens, lowering his tone. "You know Annie Lennox, don't you? Another great Scottish artist who is currently doing well in her solo career. I could build you up to be as big as her, if not bigger. However, you MUST do it on your own. Why don't you come back to my house after dinner and we can discuss things further?"

Liz grimaced as Hitchens winked at her. "You're asking me to break up my band, MY FAMILY?" cried Liz. "I am a multi instrumentalist and occasional backing vocalist at best. I have no desire to do that kind of work as, unlike the amazing Ms Lennox, I am not a naturally good singer. Please trust me when I say I know my limits. Anyway, I am loyal to my bandmates and to Joe. I wouldn't be where I am if it wasn't for them and I am NOT about to betray them."

"Look at it as a promotion rather than a betrayal," leered Hitchens. "So many doors could open for a sexy, talented young woman like you. You are a very strong woman and a go-getter. I really need more like you. Come with me and I will make you great."

Liz felt Hitchens rub his hand up the inside of her thigh. Disgusted, she threw her champaign in his face and stormed out of the restaurant to flag down a cab to take her home.

Meanwhile, back at their mansion, Moose was finishing his workout. He had worked harder than normal as he tried to take his mind off what was going on that night. As he finished showering in the downstairs bathroom, he realised that his bandmates hadn't repaced the towels.

"Damn it," Moose thought as he walked, naked, into the kitchen to make himself coffee before bed. He wasn't expecting his bandmates home for hours yet. Just then, Liz let herself in quietly and walked past the kitchen to see Moose, who was still in his state of complete undress. She smiled and blushed as she enjoyed what she was seeing as the kitchen lights highlighted his rippling, muscular body. Embarrassed, Moose grabbed a dinner plate to preserve his modesty as he apologised profusely.

"It's OK," Liz giggled. "I'll make the coffee and let you get sorted."

Once the pair got changed and settled down for coffee and the live boxing match on TV, Moose asked Liz about her date and why she was home so early.

"Moose, it wasn't a date," Liz said as she rolled her eyes. "It was a business meeting and I was trying to secure a deal for us. I thought you knew that? Anyway, it was a non-starter."

"So you're not seeing him again?" pressed Moose.

"Nope," exclaimed Liz. "It was never my intention and that's one less greasy creep for us to deal with in the future."

Liz cuddled up to Moose on the sofa and rested her head on his chest as she had often done for the past year. He was a lot happier and relaxed than she had seen him all day and it wasn't long until he had fallen asleep, still smiling. Liz continued to watch him as he slept. She had had feelings for Moose for a long time now but just felt she couldn't do anything about it. After all, he and the rest of the guys had watched her grow up and her transition from and awkward, frumpy school child to a strong, confident woman. She imagined that anything beyond friendship would be out of the question. Right now he looked adorable with his long, dark, curly hair and lightly tanned skin. He looked angelic as he lay peacefully on the sofa and Liz decided to steal a kiss. However, to her horror, he woke up.

"I'm sorry," Liz gulped as she thought Moose would be angry.

To her surprise, he lifted her on top of him and continued to kiss her. This was the first time she had really been kissed and it felt like nothing she had ever felt in her short life. It was a sensation of a combination of heat and electricity surging through her entire body as they continued to kiss and remove each other's clothes. There was no turning back now. They headed through to Liz's bedroom where Liz would lose her virginity. Everything felt so right and Liz regretted nothing.

Liz was woken the following morning by shouting

which she could hear from the living room directly below her bedroom. She got showered, dressed and went down to see what all the noise was about. Angel was shouting, very angrily, at Moose in very fast Italian. Moose nodded and smiled as his young brother got into his personal space and continued to shout at him, his face red and contorted with rage. Moose would occasionally smile at Carl, who sat in the huge, leather armchair laughing hysterically at whatever obscenities Angel was shouting. Debbie and Ronnie sat at the dining table quietly eating breakfast with their heads down as they tried to mind their own business. Leonora, the little, middle-aged housekeeper, put a hand on Angel's shoulder as she tried to diffuse the situation.

"Maybe he was only using the shower, baby," Leonora gently whispered to him in Italian.

"No, he DID NOT just have a shower. Maybe a GOLDEN one," shouted Angel, angrily, in English before continuing to yell at his brother in Italian.

"OK," Moose shouted back at Angel. "How about we remember our manners and continue this conversation in English? If you must know I enjoyed my night last night, just like you enjoyed your own night whoring and touring on the tiles. I am hoping to make a go of things with Liz and I am happier than I have been in a long time. Now, if you'll excuse the Hell out of me, I have training to do."

"What's going on?" asked Liz.

The living room was now deathly silent. Moose said goodbye to Debbie, Ronnie, Carl and Leonora before kissing Liz goodbye, telling her he loved her and that he would see her later.

"Shocking. Just shocking," Angel said to Liz, angrily before storming out after his brother. "How could you let him do that to you? You realise you're just going to be another notch on that slut's bedpost, don't you? Don't say you weren't bloody warned!"

Moose and Liz laugh as they remember Angel's reaction to it all. "He was always so protective of you," says Moose.

"He was indeed," smiles Liz. "You all were. I am a very lucky woman."

She puts her coffee cup down and tries for a kiss. Moose doesn't resist and, before they know it, they are having full-on, energetic sex on the sofa just as they had done many times in their younger days. The spark is still there, even after all the years they have been apart.

The couple have lost track of time and the sun is beginning to set as they lie relaxing in each other's arms.

"By the way," says Moose. "What is the story with Angel?"

"He has, somehow, got it into his head that he raped me on the night of the farewell gig," sighs Liz.

"Jesus," gasps Moose. "Is that the reason he has been hiding for all these years? He would NEVER have done anything to harm you. He always believed it was his duty to protect you seeing as how he wanted you to join the band from day one."

"Moose, I know that and so do you. It took a lot for me to convince him that it never happened but I'm glad he has finally accepted the truth and is settled down now," replies Liz.

"I should never have left him," Moose says sorrowfully. "I thought, with all his good fortune, he would have been able to get help for himself but there are far more predators out there who only see dollar signs, ready to take advantage of vulnerable celebrities than there are people who genuinely want to help. I, honestly, didn't think he needed me anymore. I didn't think any of you did. How could I have been so naive?"

Liz looks up at Moose, who is now quiet, to see that he is crying. It is the first time she has ever seen her tough boyfriend shed tears.

"You weren't to know, babe," soothes Liz. "None of that was your fault and you were never expected to bear the brunt of everything. As I said before, you and I didn't have any easy decisions around that time. You were taking care of Ronnie and you couldn't be in two places at once. I knew exactly what it was like out there. That was why I left and I hoped Angel would have done the same after leaving hospital. Obviously, the drug dealers were lying in wait and got to him first. Thankfully, he is in a far better place now and it can only get better from here."

Moose takes a few moments to compose himself.

"The three of us have one more thing to do," says Liz. "Tomorrow, we go for a drive to your mum's house."

"No, not tomorrow," says Moose nervously as he dries his tears.

"Come on, Moose," encourages Liz. "There's no time like the present. You and Angel have no idea how blessed you are to still have your mum. The love is still there even though she has seen neither of you for twenty years. I lost my own beautiful mum when I was just six years old and not a day goes by when I don't think about her. Please come with me tomorrow and make up for lost time. Your mum is not angry and she is not going to grill you on where you have been. She just wants to know you're alright and to see you."

"Liz McLarnon," says Moose quietly. "I love you so much."

"I love you too, baby," replies Liz as she kisses him goodnight. "Angel and I will pick you up tomorrow at 10 a.m."

Liz arrives home to find the rest of her bandmates, Debbie and Caitlin all chilling out and drinking coffee in the living room. They had all been having a jam session, practising old songs and discussing new material while Liz had been gone. Debbie and Caitlin had even moved their equipment into Liz's music room. Liz smiles as it reminds her of old times. After more reminiscing and discussing future plans with Liz, the members bid Liz and Angel goodnight as they leave for home.

Liz stands behind Angel and massages his shoulders as she tells him the plan for tomorrow.

"Tomorrow?" he gasps as his eyes widen. "Liz, I don't think I'm ready for that."

"Come on, Angel," Liz assures him. "You have nothing to dread. Your mum only wants to know that you and Moose are both alright. I promise you, she's not angry."

"I've not seen Mom since well before our last gig," Angel says as he hangs his head, trying to fight back the tears. "My drug problem was spiralling out of control and I didn't want to take that to her doorstep. When I lost my fortune and couldn't get a job, I didn't want to go to her house with nothing. Then there was that incident I thought happened with you. Mom loved you like one of her own..."

"It's alright, big bro," whispers Liz. "Come on. To bed with you. It's getting late and we have an early rise and a long drive in the morning."

The following morning Liz, Moose and Angel arrive at a well-maintained cottage in the countryside which is familiar to all three of them. The guys are extremely nervous as they walk several paces behind Liz as she knocks on the door. There stands an elegant lady in her eighties. Maria's jet black hair that Moose and Angel remember is now silvery white but she appears to be strong and in very good health. She always had been a strong, independant woman since being widowed at a young age when the boys' father was killed in an industrial accident, leaving Maria to bring up young Mario and Angelo on her own. She didn't marry again until her sons had left home and were well in their twenties. Sadly, Maria was widowed again fifteen years ago having suddenly lost her second husband to a fatal heart attack.

"Hello, Maria," Liz greets her as she hugs her. "I have a surprise for you today."

Moose and Angel round the corner. "My babies," Maria gasps and runs to them, hugging them both.

Liz sits quietly crying with happiness on the bench

outside the cottage, allowing Maria alone time with her sons that she had neither seen nor heard from in such a long time. It really is an emotional time for all of them. Maria had often dreamed of seeing her sons again and it was now finally happening.

Liz drives them to the classy Italian, family-run restaurant where she and Maria had frequented since they had reconnected fourteen years ago. It feels like a proper family day out as they all chat about old times, what Moose and Angel had been doing, what they are doing now and, of course, the future of the band now that they are all reunited. Liz hasn't seen Maria this happy since she moved back to the U.S. Maria is also thrilled at the prospect of Moose and Liz getting back together.

Liz casts her mind back to Amber. She would need to get another meeting with her soon, mainly to thank her very much for all she had done for her and her bandmates. She also has no doubt in her mind that her father and Papa Joe would be working hard behind the scenes trying to get the band back on the road again.

Chapter 10:
Preparing For The Comeback

It has been a very busy week since Amber's sensational interview with Hell Freeze. Her audience is ecstatic at the prospect of the band reforming and are excited to learn of the future of it. She wraps up yet another busy show and makes her way to Bikers' Nightclub having been invited by Liz for a late lunch and a chat.

Amber is greeted on arrival by Angie, who is very excited about the reforming of Hell Freeze having been the rock by Liz's side since she had been reunited with her former bandmates and ex-lover just last week.

"I just want to say a massive thank you for all you've done," Angie tells Amber. "I, honestly, don't think I've ever seen Liz this happy in all the years we have been friends."

"Thanks, Angie," beams Amber. "I'm glad to hear that, first hand, from somebody close to Liz. It's all been very rewarding and I had no idea I would get this far with this project. In fact, I don't even see it as a project anymore. I feel as though all the bandmates, crew and managers are now my friends."

"Definitely," agrees Angie. "You have gone over and above your call of duty and I hope you'll keep in touch with us when this is all over."

"I would be honoured, Angie," replies Amber. "Thank you so much."

"I can't believe it has been a week already," enthuses Amber when she sits down with Liz. "My show has been crazy busy with a wealth of your adoring fans and my management team are over the moon with this project. How have things been at your end since I last saw you?"

"Busy but, workwise, I am trying to get the guys and gals to keep the brakes on this time," replies Liz. "When I'm not here, I am either rehearsing old and new material with the guys or I'm with Moose."

"That's so good to hear," says Amber. "Moose seemed so bitter about absolutely everything and he was dead set about having nothing to do with the band. I had a feeling it was mainly because he had lost you. I'm glad he's coming round now and that you are making a go of things again."

"So am I," replies Liz. "It's great to have him back and to have a full house again."

"Liz," Amber's tone is now serious. "How has Angel been with you since he moved in?"

"Oh no," sighs Liz. "What did he tell you?"

"He told me he had done a 'real dreadful thing' when he was alone with me at the hotel but didn't get to tell me because I was interrupted," replies Amber. "I could tell by his body language that it was something to do with you as he was very on-edge at the prospect of seeing you again and when you arrived at the hotel that night. I was reluctant to leave you alone with him for that reason."

"Yes," replies Liz. "He was about to tell you he forced himself on me."

"What? No way," exclaims Amber.

"Amber," says Liz. "What Angel thought happened and what actually happened are two completely different things."

Liz continues to give Amber an account of exactly what happened on the night of their final gig, from when she helplessly watched her sick bandmates perform until she had no choice but to leave Angel at the hospital to be treated for his drug overdose, not knowing if he would survive.

"Poor Angel," says Amber. "He is such a lovely person and he thinks the world of you, although not in that way. He was almost bursting with pride when he was talking about your audition and how he, Ronnie and Moose won their decision to keep you."

"I know," replies Liz. "He has NEVER thought of me in that way and he has certainly never made any advances towards me, even when he had a drink in him. At one point, we were sharing a tiny bedroom and he had every opportunity to try something then as Moose left at dark o'clock for work most mornings. There would have been no witnesses and it would have been my word against his. I'm just glad he finally believes me and is taking care of himself again."

"I am so delighted for all of you," smiles Amber.

"Me too," says Liz. "I never thought I would work with the guys like before any time soon but here we are. All five of us have actually written songs while we were away and look forward to recording some of them. You are more than welcome to swing by my place anytime and we'll do another interview and give you a taster of what we have coming up next."

"That would be awesome," cries Amber. "Thanks

so much, Liz."

"Thank YOU from myself and the guys too," replies Liz. "Thanks to you, Hell Freeze are on their way back. I'll touch base with you again when I have news from my managers on upcoming gigs."

The following days roll into weeks as the band have daily rehearsal dates at Liz's house between their regular jobs. The bandmates, Debbie and Caitlin are having so much fun preparing for their upcoming gigs that they forget the time. Even Papa Joe and Big Tam have lost track of time as they organise the band's gigs for the months ahead.

It is a Saturday morning and Liz has risen early for her run. She is just finishing up when Moose arrives, having taken the rest of the day off work to spend some time with her before getting tore into rehearsals. As Angel is still fast asleep, they go to Liz's bedroom for some alone time while they wait for Carl and Ronnie to arrive. Liz notices that Moose is quieter than usual as they both lie in bed chilling out but she doesn't question it.

Carl and Papa Joe arrive shortly afterwards. Although Papa Joe is his usual cheery self, there is something different about Carl and it's not good. Ronnie is very quiet too as he sips on his coffee trying to keep himself awake. Even Debbie is struggling to keep her eyes open as she rests her head on Caitlin's shoulder. Angel eventually joins his bandmates, looking very dishevelled and still yawning even after a cold shower. The room is unusually quiet as Papa Joe talks, excitedly, about the various venues the band are due to perform at.

Big Tam makes his entrance having been dropped off by his youngest son John. "Hello, superstars!," he sings jovially as he waves his walking stick. "How are my young yins doing today?"

"Shattered, man," mumbles Ronnie.

"Burst," Carl chimes in.

"Done in," says Debbie, shaking her head.

"Dead," yawns Angel as he closes his eyes and leans against Carl.

"Fucked," groans Moose as he sprawls across Liz's lap.

"For crying out loud, kids," exclaims Tam. "You're like a bloody sack of tatties and I bet I know why!"

With all her might, Liz sits Moose up and jumps to her feet. "So do I," she shouts. "Can anyone remember the last time we had a day off?"

The bandmates, Debbie and Caitlin all look at each other confused and now very much awake.

"I'll tell you," says Liz as she sits on the arm of her father's chair. "Six bloody weeks ago. Six weeks of solid rehearsals over and above our own jobs! Guys and gals, we promised we wouldn't do that again and here we are!"

"Six weeks?" asks Carl, surprised. "Are you sure?"

"Aye," shouts Liz. "A gentle reminder that we're not young anymore and we need to pace ourselves. Our days of dousing the candle in petrol and setting it alight should be over!"

"Shut up, Liz," laughs Moose. "Speak for yourself, you old hag."

"Moose, if I rise…," Liz warns.

"It won't be by much," shouts Ronnie before covering

his mouth as the room erupts with laughter at his unexpected cheek.

"Right," continues Liz. "I am the doctor in the house and you guys are going to listen!"

"You tell them, Auntie Liz," exclaims Caitlin.

"Honestly, Caitlin," continues Liz, in her matter-of-fact tone. "This was what triggered everybody's demons before. It started off with a tiny bit of speed and a couple of beers to get them through rehearsals and gigs, then it was lines of coke. Before we knew it, it was heroin and other hard drugs. I don't want those people at my door again and I certainly DO NOT want the demons they leave behind."

The room is silent.

"OK, I'm done," smiles Liz. "I'll get off my soap box now. School's out for today as well as tomorrow. You are more than welcome to come over for a blether or to use the gym and hot tub as my door is always open but absolutely nothing work related. We owe it to ourselves. Is that fair enough?"

"Well said, little sister," exclaims Debbie.

"Right," Liz claps her hands and goes back to her seat. "I'll hand you over to management for our rundown of upcoming gigs. Dad and Papa Joe, it's over to you."

Papa Joe and Big Tam give an account of what has been organised so far, with the first gig being six weeks away that very day.

"How are you young 'uns fixed fixed for this?" asks Papa Joe.

"You know what?" says Angel, who is on his feet. "I think we're as ready as we're ever going to be."

"Definitely," exclaims Moose, as he playfully wrestles his brother to the floor as the rest of the band, Debbie and Caitlin laugh.

"So it's decided then?" beams Liz. "We need a good dinner to celebrate. Let's stay here and chill for a bit and I will phone Angie and let her know we're calling into Bikers' later."

"Let's invite Amber too," suggests Moose. "All of this is possible because of her and it's her pet project that she'll be keen to publicise on her show."

"Good shout, babe," says Liz. "We owe her big for this."

"If my book sales are anything to go by, I have a feeling these gigs are going to be a sell-out," smiles Carl, rubbing his hands with glee.

"OK," says Liz as she lowers her tone again. "Just a gentle reminder to keep the brakes on."

Liz gets on the phone to Angie.

"Hey, Louise," sings Liz as Angie answers. "It was just to give you the heads up that I'll be calling in later on with the guys, Debbie and Caitlin."

"A word of advice, Thelma," replies Angie with a serious tone. "Don't."

"What's wrong?" asks Liz. "Has there been trouble?"

"Wrong, Thelma?" cries Angie. "Everything is exactly right! It has been crazy busy because of the news of you guys reforming. We are constantly awash with Hell Freeze fans hoping to rub shoulders with you and the guys. I hope you don't mind but I had to take on twelve extra staff, including security, to cope with the demand."

"God no, Louise, of course not," laughs Liz. "That's

great news! I don't know what to say. I am just stunned!"

"Thelma if you'll allow me I'll have Laura, Chris and their team prepare you some food and send it over to you," says Angie. "Trust me. It's for your own safety."

"Thanks, Louise," replies Liz as she concludes the phone call. "Love you loads."

"Unbelievable," exclaims Liz as she hangs up the phone. "Good news fair travels fast!"

As the weeks go on, Amber's show has never been busier as she updates her audience on added tour dates due to popular demand and giveaways as Papa Joe and Big Tam had donated tickets for gigs at selected venues the band were due to perform at. She does, however, make a point of contacting Derek at Moonlight Laundry Services and awarding him a pair of tickets for his original idea of tracing and reuniting Hell Freeze.

Amber calls Liz to update her on ticket sales and they are amazed to discover that all their upcoming gigs have sold out already.

"This is so exciting" cheers Liz. "Amber, would you please do us the honour of being at some of our gigs and coming backstage with us? You are more than welcome to bring your parents to any that suit them. Your Mum can meet Angel."

Amber shrieks with delight. What originally seemed an impossible task is now reality and Liz, her very first girl crush is speaking to Amber first hand as though she is a close friend.

"Liz, I would love that!," cries Amber. "Mom will be

delighted although I think my dad will be jealous."

"That's OK," laughs Liz. "I'm sure a wee sparring match with my Moose will take his mind off it."

Chapter 11:
Full-Time Commitment

The band are now counting down their last four weeks until their very first gig in twenty years. The bandmates, engineers and management team have not felt excitement like it in such a long time.

Moose and Liz are enjoying some alone time at Moose's apartment when their peace is interrupted by a knock at the door.

"Ignore it," sighs Moose as he wraps the duvet around his shoulders.

"No, it sounds urgent," says Liz. "You'd better go and see what that is, just in case."

Moose groans as he gets up and throws on a pair of jogging bottoms and a tee shirt and is surprised to see his landlord standing at the door. He would usually call to say he is coming for an inspection so this must be a surprise one.

"Good morning, Stan," Moose greets him. "Come on in."

"Good morning, Mario," replies Stan. "I'm afraid I can't stay as I am in a bit of a hurry. I noticed your car parked outside so I thought I would come and break it to you sooner rather than later."

"What's happened?" asks Moose.

"I'm really sorry there is no easy way to tell you this," says Stan, nervously. "Rita and I are moving to Spain and we have decided to sell our properties. I hate doing this to you, Mario. You have been such a good tenant and I know you have carried out numerous repairs for me since you took on the lease."

"Stan, it's fine," replies Moose, calmly. "I'll clear out my things by the end of the week. Please let me know if you and your good lady need me to help you with anything."

Stan is surprised that Moose has taken the news so well. He smiles as she shakes Moose's hand, thanking him for his business over the years before bidding him goodbye.

"It's alright, babe," smiles Liz. "You're at mine most of the time now anyway and the rent for this place is a hole in your bank account you don't need. We might as well pack the rest of your things now."

As the weeks go on, the band continue to get together for practice sessions between Moose and Ronnie's shifts. The bandmates are having a coffee break when Ronnie gets a phone call. He looks solemn as he leaves the room to continue his conversation in private. A little while later, Ronnie enters the room smiling.

"I've just been offered a retirement package," he says with delight. "It's happened at just the right time because it means I can free myself up for rehearsals and gigs."

"Congratulations, honey," cheers Debbie. "When do you finish up?"

"They want me to go in and discuss it tomorrow but the boss said it will be the end of next month," replies Ronnie. "I'LL BE A FREE MAN AND FULL-TIME ROCKER! I can commit full time to the band now."

"Sorry to be the wet blanket here," says Liz. "Please remember we are still pacing ourselves. Just because you've retired and Moose and Angel are living here doesn't mean we go mad. I still want you, Debbie and Caitlin to have your days off. By the way... congratulations, pal."

Everyone cheers and congratulates Ronnie on his new freedom as they decide to wrap rehearsals up for the night and have some food and drinks to celebrate. The bandmates are enjoying their evening when there is an unexpected knock at the door. Liz answers the door to see her gentle giant brother, John, who appears very upset.

"Liz, I'm sorry to drop by like this," says John as he tries to fight back tears. "I mentioned to Alec, in the passing, that Da had a fall now he and Jimmy have taken him to Scotland and put him in a home. I'm so sorry, pal. I feel as though I've let you down."

"Please don't worry, John," Liz assures him. "You were doing a champion job and it was inevitable that my dad was going to have the odd fall due to his Parkinson's. A nursing home though? Dad's not ready for that. I don't know what Alec and Jimmy are thinking! He'll lose his mind!"

"That's what scares me," replies John. "Since you and the guys got together and Da started getting involved again, I've not seen him this full of life since he retired."

"I know, right?" exclaims Liz "John, the guys and I are about to go on tour and we really need Dad. Leave it to me. I'm going to Scotland to get him back and, in the mean time, I have another job offer for you to think about."

"What's that?" asks John. "I've been a nurse all my days and I don't know anything else."

"John, the guys and I need a strong, reliable roady who can drive the bus when we're on tour," says Liz. "Would you be up for that? We will pay you well."

"Oh, God, Aye!," beams John. "All those free shows with my favourite rock band ever!"

"Welcome aboard, big bro," smiles Liz as she high fives him. "I just need to fly out tomorrow and sort these two terrors out. Which home is my dad in?"

"I don't know, pal," replies John. "I was so upset that I never even thought to ask. I know Harry was taking Anna to Greece for a break and he would NEVER have allowed this. The best person to ask is Hugh. Nothing gets past him."

Liz gets on the phone to her brother Hugh.

"Hiya, wee pal," Hugh greets her. "How's tricks?"

"I'm good, thanks, Hugh," replies Liz. "More importantly, how are you and Cathy?"

"All good here too, thanks, pal," says Hugh. "Listen, what's the story with my da? Has he deteriorated as much as Alec and Jimmy are saying? I was going to see him tonight and..."

"No, Hugh," interrupts Liz. "I got back with my band, we are about to go on a comeback tour and my dad and Papa Joe have been managing us. He has never been this fit or sharp in a long time. He had a daft wee fall because he and John got a new carpet but he wasn't hurt. I am bloody raging at Alec and Jimmy! I need to get my dad out of there."

"Oh totally," agrees Hugh. "Right, hen, Cathy and I

will call in and see my da tonight. When you arrive in Glasgow, come straight to mine and we'll get things organised from there."

"Thanks, Hugh," replies Liz. "You're an absolute diamond."

As soon as Liz arrives in Glasgow the next day, she heads straight for the nursing home where Hugh had said their father was. Liz is met by her brothers, Alec and Jimmy at the entrance.

"Hiya darling," says Alec, surprised. "How are you, wee sis?"

"Don't 'darling' me," says Liz, angrily. "What are you two playing at?"

"Come on, Liz," says Jimmy. "We heard about my da's fall and didn't think our John was up for the job anymore so we thought we would bring him here to keep an eye on him seeing as how Alec's retired and I'm hoping for my early shot soon."

"So you never thought to consult me?" scolds Liz.

"We know you're a busy woman, love, and we thought John needed a break," replies Alec. "That's all."

"I'm not so busy that I can't make time for my dad," says Liz. "John was doing a fantastic job and Wullie, Tommy and Robert are always at his house too. I also think you have all forgotten who my dad REALLY is! He's as strong as an ox with a mind like a steel trap. Honestly, he's not any less of a man because he has Parkinson's. Guys, I'm taking my dad home. He can move in with me where he will always have company. I promise you, he will be looked after and you two are more than welcome to come for a holiday any time you want. I need ALL my family with me at this time."

"You have our full support, our Liz," says Jimmy as he picks her up and whirls her around.

"Thanks, guys," beams Liz. "I'm taking my dad to Hugh's just now. Why don't you two come out for dinner with us and ask Mary and Ellen to come along? We'll make a night of it!"

Alec laughs and shakes his head. "Good God, hen," he puffs. "When did you get so tough? You are exactly how I remember my ma. All you need is the long, curly hair."

"Wee Mary," sighs Liz. "I miss that wee soul and if I could be a fraction of the woman she was..."

"Believe me, our Liz, you ARE," exclaims Alec.

Liz is taken to her father's room by a member of care staff.

"He's been in his room all day, refused to go to bed for my colleagues last night, he won't come out and is refusing to eat or even take a cup of tea," the care worker informs her. "We've tried but we can't make him."

"I am so sorry," Liz apologises. "He's a tough cookie. I'll talk to him."

Liz pops her head round the door to see her father sitting on a chair just staring into space.

"Hiya, dad," says Liz, quietly.

"Hello, my wee lamb," says Big Tam. He is smiling but it's not his usual bright smile that emphasises his piercing blue eyes. "I can't believe you came all this way to see your old dad."

"That's not why I'm here, dad," replies Liz. "I didn't

want this for you and I've come to get you. We're going home."

"What?" asks Tam, surprised.

"Alec and Jimmy got it wrong, dad," explains Liz. "If OK with you, I want you to come back with me to the States. Dad, the guys and I need you in our corner. We are about to blow up big again and Papa Joe needs his strong partner in crime."

"My wee love," smiles Tam as he wipes away tears. "I knew I could rely on you."

"Dad, how many times have you done it for me?" asks Liz. "Mum died the week I was due to start school yet you supported all nine of us and made sure we got to school, college and uni, you took me to the U.S so you could make a better life for me along with the boys who wanted to go, you supported me when I decided to leave school to become a rock star, you stood by myself and the guys through all our setbacks and you gave Moose and I your blessing despite all the raised eyebrows. I could go on."

"What did I do to deserve you, hen?" beams Tam, now with his full genuine smile back.

"Let's go, Dad," says Liz as she takes her father by the arm. "Alec and Jimmy are waiting for us to take us to Hugh's. Please don't be mad at them. They thought they were doing right and I have already bollocked them."

"You're getting more like your ma every day, wee yin," laughs Tam as they make their way to the car.

"I couldn't have asked for a better family, dad," says Liz. "I love you, boss, but I'm going to tell you what I told the guys and gals: BREAKS ON!"

"Right you are, hen," laughs Tam as he puts his arm around Liz's shoulders.

Chapter 12:
The Hell Freeze Survival Tour Begins

The day has finally arrived for Hell Freeze to go on tour. The morning of this particular tour is a far cry from how Liz remembers that of their farewell tour twenty years ago. It is 11 a.m, she has just finished her workout with Moose and Angel and they are settling down for a light snack before the rest of their entourage arrives. Everyone is relaxed and in high spirits having taken on Liz's advice on slowing down and making time for themselves. Apart from the very occasional alcoholic beverage to relax after rehearsals at night time, the bandmates are clean and sober and looking forward to putting on the top class performance their loyal fans have waited so long for.

The management team, bandmates and engineers have worked hard over the past few months in order to make their comeback tour a success. Their hard work was already showing because their first gig had to be moved forward in order to make room for the added dates at that same venue due to the demand from adoring fans.

Liz thinks back to the morning of the final gig of their farewell tour. She had risen late, with a blinding headache after yet another broken sleep due to severe malnutrition. She had really wanted to go to the hospital with Ronnie to give him some moral support as he went to visit Debbie and baby Caitlin, unsure at this stage whether or not he would ever be able to bring either his wife of his daughter home. Ronnie later confessed that he had checked in on Liz before leaving but found that she was fast asleep and too weak and ill to cope with such a traumatic hospital visit. Carl and Angel were already drunk, it was only 10.30 a.m and this was just for starters. They went on to take much harder stuff later on. As Liz went into the kitchen for some paracetamol, Moose offered her some breakfast without even looking at her to which she had refused. She was unable to eat or even take a glass of water as she knew she would bring it straight back up again. She didn't get the same high when she weighed herself and the scale showed yet another loss. She couldn't even confide in her father because he was already attending to her brother Hugh, who was critically ill following his accident. Liz had contemplated abandoning the gig in favour of a flight home with her father to visit her beloved older brother but her father had encouraged her to attend the gig as "we owe it to the fans".

Liz snaps back to reality when she receives a phone call. "Hiya, pal," she smiles cheerily as she answers. "Thanks for doing this. Yep, we'll be there soon. See ya. Love you loads."

She gets off the couch, looks out of the window and smiles as Angel is relaxing as he plays his guitar and sings to himself.

"Angel, my darling," smiles Liz. "Can you put your guitar down for a few minutes?"

Angel looks confused but he does it anyway. Liz

takes him by the hand and guides him towards the window.

"What the Hell are you doing, Liz?" asks Angel, startled. "Moose is only in the bath!"

"Relax," whispers Liz. "You've stayed here for a good few months now and I've never told you how proud I am of you, big bro."

"Liz, where are you going with this?" asks Angel. "What have I done except take up space in your house and eat your food? I don't even have a job so I can put something towards rent."

Liz rolls her eyes. "Angel, you DO have a job. You've barely had a guitar out of your hands since you came home and I've enjoyed lots of delicious Italian cuisine since you moved in," replies Liz. "Anyway I was thinking, earlier on, about how different things are right now compared to how they were for our farewell gig all those years ago. Angel, I thought I had lost you. Now you are clean, sober and you have been in the gym with Moose nearly every day. You're in better shape now than you were before your drug addiction and you've not even had a cigarette."

"I've not had one of those things since the day you made me stop," laughs Angel.

He recalls the time he smoked a cigarette for the very last time. The four male bandmates were away for a boys' weekend which comprised of camping, hunting, fishing and drinking. While they were away, 17-year-old Liz confided in Debbie that she still felt ugly and insecure despite losing weight and getting fit as she trained consistently with Moose and Marco. As the guys came home on the Sunday evening and settled down, Liz bounced into the living room and revealed her new rock chic look. Her hair was cropped and dyed peroxide blonde, she wore make-up for the first time in her life, she sported a leather jacket, figure-hugging black jeans and thigh-high stiletto boots. Her cheeks puffed out as she blew on a lit cigarette without inhaling.

"What the Hell are you doing?" Angel shouted at her as he grabbed the cigarette out of her hand and stubbed it out in the ash tray. "That is a disgusting, filthy habit that will kill you! What are your father and brothers going to say when they see you doing that and about how bad you smell?"

"Hang on, Angel," Liz shot back. "You're smoking too so don't tell me what to do."

Sure enough, Angel still had a half-smoked cigarette hanging from his mouth. He rolled his eyes as he looked around the room at the guys and at Debbie. The room had fallen silent. Angel took a long drag on his cigarette and held his breath for a good few seconds before exhaling. He stubbed out the cigarette, threw the packet with the remaining ones at Carl and told the group: "Right. That was my last cigarette."

The room erupted with all the bandmates and Debbie chanting *"Oooooooooohhhhhhhhh,"* as Angel had been known to smoke more than 40 cigarettes a day. They all sat looking at each other for about five minutes as Angel fidgeted nervously.

"How are you feeling, bro?" whispered Moose, anxiously.

"Hellish," replied Angel. "On edge, hungry, irritable, forgetful. What was it you asked me again?"

Everyone laughed.

"You've got this," cried Moose as he playfully punched his brother on the shoulder.

"You know what, bro," Ronnie chimed in as he handed his own remaining cigarettes to Carl, shook Angel's hand and winked at Debbie. "We do this together. I don't want cigarettes in the house for when the wee ones start arriving."

"Moose was right and God bless Ronnie," smiles Liz as she and Angel laugh at the memory. "You can achieve anything you want and I have a reward for you. It's an early birthday present I want you to have now. Look at this."

The pair look out of the window to see Liz's brothers, Tommy and Robert, wheeling a shiny, expensive-looking motorcycle out of their company truck.

"Please tell me you didn't," exclaims Angel as his eyes widen.

"A Harley-Davidson FLHR Road King," beams Liz as she puts the keys in his hand. "I thought you'd like her. After all, you'll need your own transport now that you are a rock star coming out of retirement."

"Liz, I can't accept this," says Angel. "It's far too much."

"Yes you can," exclaims Liz. "I have been discussing this with Tommy and Robert for weeks now and I can't give it back to them now and cost them a sale. They'll even maintain for you."

"You're too good to me," smiles Angel as he crouches down and gives Liz a kiss and a hug.

"I am so proud of you, big bro," whispers Liz. "Let's go outside and you can take her for a run."

Angel and Liz go outside and greet Liz's two brothers. Angel thanks Liz and the guys for the bike as he takes it for a test drive. Just then, a silver limousine pulls into the driveway. All three are stunned to see it is their brother Wullie with their four brothers from Scotland. Wullie wanted to surprise Liz by bringing them over to see Hell Freeze's opening gig.

"This is amazing," cries Liz, who is ecstatic at having all her siblings together again. "I'm going to phone our John and tell him to bring dad over. This gig is going to be some buzz!"

The atmosphere of Liz's mansion is electric as the rest of her bandmates, engineers, her father and Papa Joe arrive. Moose has also brought his mother along as she is proud to see her sons working together again. Also in attendance is Liz's best friend and business partner, Angie, and Moose's long-term friends Lukas and Marco. Finally, Amber arrives with her parents in tow as Liz greets them and welcomes them into her home. Liz looks at Amber's mother who looks like a very nervous, star-struck teenager.

"Have a seat, Jenna," Liz says quietly as she tries to calm her down. "I'll go and get Angel."

Liz walks into the living room with Angel.

"Angel, meet Jenna," says Liz. "She is your biggest fan."

Amber chuckles quietly to herself as it is the first time she has ever seen her mother totally speechless. Angel is more handsome in person now than Jenna remembers him as a pin-up from her young days. Better still he has a warm, caring personality and he makes time for his fans. He does an amazing job as he manages to calm Jenna down so she can chat and pose for some pictures.

Liz turns her attention to Amber's father. "Do you have your phone on you, Matt?" she asks him.

"I sure do, love," he laughs as he scoops Liz up and asks his daughter to take a picture. "Is there any chance I can get a photo with my nemesis too?"

"Certainly," laughs Liz as she calls Moose over.

Matt laughs as he finally meets Moose. Although his body is impressive and probably better than it was during the band's hay day, Matt had expected Moose to be a lot taller. Still, he is delighted to pose for some photos that look as though the two men are sparring.

As everyone is chatting over some food and drink, Liz calls for their attention as she beckons Amber over.

"Ladies and gentlemen, guys and gals, can I have your attention please?" Liz shouts above all the chat. "I would like to introduce, to all of you, this amazing young lady. This is Amber Groves who hosts Lunchtime with Amber on Golden Plus FM. She is responsible for our reunion. Without this determined young woman, none of this would be possible. Everyone, can I please propose a toast to Amber?"

Everyone raises their drinks in the air. "To Amber," they all say in unison followed by a cheer.

It is now show time. Debbie and Caitlin have set up their equipment on stage with the help of John and the bandmates are getting ready to go on stage for their first gig in twenty years. Amber is in attendance too as she is broadcasting live for her radio station. Papa Joe and Big Tam take to the stage and lift a microphone each.

"Ladies and gentlemen," Joe says as he throws his still-powerful voice to the excited audience. "Reintroducing to the world..."

"Please welcome back to the world of rock and roll," continues Tam. "The legendary HELL FREEZE!"

One by one and in order that they joined the band, the bandmates stride onto the stage confidently and take their places: Angel, Carl, Moose, Ronnie and Liz as the audience erupts into a massive round of applause.

"Good evening, beautiful people," Angel addresses the audience. "We want to say a massive thank you to all our fans, old and new, for all your support and for turning out to see our first gig in twenty years! Sit back or, better still, get up and dance and enjoy the show!"

The band opens their gig with their last ever number one single. Before they know it, a full-blown party is happening in the venue as the audience dance and sing along to all their favourite hit songs from Hell Freeze. The gig carries on for longer than the band had anticipated as the audience demands one last hit song after another. Finally, the band close the show with a massive outro with their instruments and bow to the audience, thanking them for their loyalty and support even after all this time.

After the gig, the party continues backstage as the bandmates and Amber are reunited with their loved ones. Liz observes the happy atmosphere and what a far cry it is from their final gig twenty years ago. She remembers it as being a very cold, lonely time for herself and her bandmates. Although they were together in person, they were isolated from the real world as well as family and friends in spirit. The aura backstage is now warm and healthy and everyone is in high spirits with not an intoxicated soul in sight.

Liz smiles as her beloved Moose cuddles up to her as her father, her best friend, Maria and all eight of her brothers look on with pride, something she never thought would happen again. She watches with contentment as the rest of her bandmates celebrate the roaring success of their opening gig with all the different friends and family members who had attended backstage for moral support.

The rest of the weekend continues to prove a success as all three nights see the band host very busy, action-packed shows for masses of adoring fans who had anticipated their return to the spotlight for years. All in all, it was a successful weekend and Hell Freeze are well and truly out of retirement.

Chapter 13:
Hell Freeze On Their Way Back

Following a very successful weekend, the bandmates wake the following Monday morning to find that they are featured on every channel on breakfast television as well as on the front page of most of the newspapers.

Moose picks up a well-respected broadsheet. "Look at that," he says excitedly. "We made the front page. Bloody Hell, we must have done something right at the weekend."

"You were amazing," exclaims Caitlin. "Read it out, Uncle Moose."

"'Sensational rock band of the 1990s, the legendary Hell Freeze, kicked of their Survival Tour and took the audience of a local California venue by storm as hoards of dedicated fans flocked to the the band's first performances in over twenty years'," Moose recited. "'On all three nights, the band brought the house down as they wowed their faithful followers with old and new songs. The wrinkly rockers...' GOD DAMN IT!"

Moose throws the newspaper across the room in temper and kicks over the coffee table, breaking some cups, plates and ornaments in the process.

"Moose? What the fuck?" laughs Liz.

"'Wrinkly rockers' indeed," shouts Moose angrily. "HOW DARE THEY SAY THAT ABOUT US?"

"Shocking, eh?" agrees Ronnie, who is now on his

feet and stomping around angrily.

"Moose and Ronnie," sighs Liz "Sit on your arses."

"No wonder," shouts Angel as he jumps up. "Bloody cheek!"

"I know right?" Carl chimes in.

Meanwhile, Debbie and Caitlin are laughing hysterically.

"Angel and Carl, you pair can sit on your arses as well," scolds Liz. "Good God, I didn't sign up for this!"

"No wonder," Moose continues to shout. "That comment was BANG out of order!"

"Moose it was a stupid, throw-away comment," says Liz. "A comment that probably came from a young journalist who is ages with our Caitlin and Amber. He still gave us a damn good review from what I heard you read before you threw your bloody tantrum. Anyway, I'm surprised that you guys are surprised."

"What?" asks Carl shocked.

"Put it this way," Liz continues. "We are up against teenagers and twenty-somethings in the charts. I am 41 years old now and you guys are..."

"Choose your words very carefully, woman," growls Moose.

"...a wee bit older," Liz chuckles. "Anyway you'll do what exactly, Moose?"

Moose hides behind Carl and Angel in mock horror, not daring to say anymore in front of the three strong-minded women in his company.

"You guys need to accept that you did a first class job at the weekend," enthuses Debbie. "You proved to your fans that you've still got it and it can only get better from here. If anything, you will inspire the younger blood. You only had to look at your audiences to see that there were so many young people out there as well as older fans."

"Debbie, you're right," says Moose as he puts his hands up. "Sorry."

The following morning, Moose and Liz are getting ready for their gym workout when their is an unexpected knock at the front door. Liz looks at the clock on her bedside table: 6.15 a.m. Who could that be at this un-Godly hour? She answers the door to be met by Amber, who us smiling excitedly.

"Good morning, Amber," Liz greets her. "You're out and about early. Is everything alright?"

"Aaww, Liz and Moose," Amber begins. "I have the BEST news and I wanted you guys to hear it first. You guys have gone STRAIGHT IN at number three in the charts with 'Demons'!"

"NO," cries Moose.

"YES," replies Amber. "I am absolutely delighted for you. I knew you guys would be in high demand when you stepped back on-stage."

"Oh my God," gasps Liz.

"YES," cries Moose as he picks Amber up and whirls her round as she hugs him back.

"This is just the beginning," enthuses Amber. "Your single will most likely climb to number one in the next couple of weeks too."

Chapter 14:
Full Circle

The next few weeks pass in a blur as Hell Freeze continue to enjoy the popularity of their comeback tour as well as their single 'Demons', co-written by Angel and Carl, reaching number one in the U.S and U.K charts just as Amber had predicted.

The day of the final gig of the Survival Tour is now upon the band. Hell Freeze are playing in the exact same venue they played in twenty years ago for the final gig of their farewell tour. Angel and Carl can barely remember the gig but Liz, Moose and Ronnie have vivid memories of it and are happy that tonight is going to be very different to what it was all those years ago and they are looking forward to it.

Liz is enjoying a relaxing walk with Ronnie, Debbie and Caitlin as they reminisce about old times. They reflect on how thankful they are to be working together as a band again, determined to do things better than they did the first time around now that they are older and definitely wiser.

The four of them walk into the living room to find that Big Tam and Moose are face-to-face with each other, looking as though they are about to get into a fight, with Moose having his back to them. At 6 ft 4, Big Tam towers over Moose who is just 5 ft 10. However with Moose being the fitness fanatic that he is, he has the athletic physique of a much younger man. If those two got into a fist fight, it would not be a pretty sight! One of the men is heard saying "SSHHH" as they back away from each other.

"What's going on," asks Liz startled.

"Nothing, babe. Your dad and I were just talking. It's all good," says Moose as he kisses her and heads for the gym.

"Dad?" asks Liz. "Did you two just have a row? It looked, to me, like you and Moose were squaring up to each other."

"Of course not, my wee lamb," laughs Tam. "Anyway, love, this is a big day for you. You should be relaxing. Do you really think your old dad would do that to your boyfriend?"

"I don't know, Dad," laughs Liz. "You're a Partick boy who worked on the shipyards and I'm your only daughter. You're capable of all kinds of mischief..."

"Come on, pal," says Ronnie, guiding Liz out of the living room as Tam continues to smile cheekily and gives Ronnie the hush sign when Liz isn't looking. "You're reading too much into this. Let's go and get Debbie to do your make-up."

It is 7 p.m and the band are preparing to go on stage for the final gig of their come-back tour. Just like before, Papa Joe and Big Tam introduce the band to the excited audience.

Liz takes her place behind her keyboard kit as she remembers the last time she sat in this very spot twenty years ago under very different circumstances. She scans the stage looking at every one of her bandmates. Angel and Carl are in high spirits and are looking fitter and healthier than Liz has ever seen them. Ronnie is content and proud knowing that his beautiful family are working nearby as they make the production of the gig as smooth as possible. Finally, her beloved Moose is happy and relaxed as he smiles warmly at Liz throughout the gig. Liz is also content knowing that her she will be meeting up with all eight of her brothers for a catch-up tomorrow as her four eldest have made the trip from Scotland especially.

In the audience, there are other people that Liz recognises. In the front row and within touching distance of Liz is an elderly lady who is accompanied by a woman who looks to be around Liz's age. The older lady waves at Liz and the younger of the two smiles and winks when they realise they have her attention but Liz cannot, for the life of her, think how she knows these women. Both women are smiling with pride and give Liz the thumbs up throughout the gig.

The band are now half way through the gig.

"Ladies and gentlemen," Angel addresses the audience as the bandmates continue to play their instruments. "Angel Mancini reintroducing to the world HELL FREEZE. My partner in crime and our very own hit man who keeps the rhythm going: MR CARL MARTINEZ. Founding member and master of guitar riffs and our tough outer shell: MOOSE. Our oracle from the Scottish Highlands providing our bass: MR RONNIE BUCHANAN. "Also from Scotland, our godmother of soul: DR LIZ MCLARNON."

Each band member join Angel centre stage as their

name is called.

"Special thanks to our management team: MR JOSE MARTINEZ and MR THOMAS MCLARNON," Angel continues. "We are taking this quick break to thank you all so much for your loyalty and for coming back to us. We hope you are enjoying our work so far and hope you enjoy the rest of the gig. We want to see you DANCE!"

The crowd cheers as band open the second half of their gig with one of their old songs, originally intended as a solo but it had become a duet when Rick Hammer, lead singer of another massive rock band Molten Rock had joined them on-stage. Angel had felt his nose was put out of joint and the other bandmates were angry at the time but the stunt proved to go in the band's favour as Angel continued to be a good sport and sang along as a duet anyway as the audience erupted in a massive round of applause. Better still, it was the duet version of that particular song that had gone straight into the U.S and U.K charts at number one as Hammer invited the band to his studio to record it. The members of Hell Freeze were grateful for this experience as Molten Rock were such a successful band who were massive in the sixties and were still going strong.

Angel is singing his solo piece of the intended duet when suddenly, the familiar, tall, slender figure of a man in his seventies emerges from back stage with a microphone in his hand to join Angel.

Angel stops singing mid-word. "Oh my God, as I live and breath," he gasps. "Ladies and gentlemen, SIR RICK HAMMER!"

The audience roars with delight as Rick bows to them, high-fives Angel and the two rock legends continue to sing as a duet as though they are old friends as the rest of the band continue to play and look on with pride. The duo finish up and Rick Hammer shakes Angel's hand.

"Welcome back, son," beams Rick. "We are all proud of you guys."

Rick Hammer exits the stage and continues to watch Hell Freeze perform the rest of their set from the wings with his bandmates.

The end of the gig is now upon the band as all the members play the massive outro of their instruments and finishing in unison to a massive, roaring cheer from the audience. "Thank you so much, beautiful people," Angel addresses the band's devotees. "Thank you, so much, from all of us for being there for us, for coming back to us and making our band what we are. Love you all. Please take good care, stay safe and we'll see you all again very soon. KEEP ON ROCKIN'. GOOD NIGHT AND GOD BLESS."

"Ladies and gentlemen," Moose chimes in through his ear piece. "Before you all go, I would like to attempt one final stunt for you to witness. Are there any first aiders in the house tonight?"

"I've got you, big chap," John calls out from the wings, having taken on the role as first aider as well as his other duties, as he emerges with Papa Joe, Big Tam and two volunteers.

"Ladies and gentlemen," Moose continues. "The last time I attempted this stunt, TWENTY YEARS AGO, I fell on my arse. I will need all the help I can get if I fail again."

The concert hall is silent as the audience watches in anticipation. What is Moose up to and can he still pull off the stunts that he could manage twenty years ago?

"Hold this for me, bro," he says to Angel as he shoves his guitar into his brother's free hand.

"Aw, Christ, I can't watch," says Angel as he buries his face in Ronnie's shoulder. "If he breaks his neck doing a back flip..."

"Liz McLarnon," Moose smiles as he drops to one knee and opens a small box to reveal a solitaire diamond engagement ring. "Will you marry me?"

"Oh my God, AYE," Liz laughs as she pulls Moose up by the hand.

"Ladies and gentlemen," Moose shouts excitedly. "She has only gone and said YES!"

The crowd goes wild as Moose does an impressive back flip, picks Liz up, whirls her round and kisses her as his bandmates, management team and crew cheer. Even Molten Rock join the band on-stage to congratulate them on their come-back and, of course, the happy couple on their engagement.

"Come here, ya big dafty," Tam says to Moose as he embraces his future son-in-law "Congratulations, son. Look after my wee girl, will you?"

"Tam," Moose says with a half smile. "Do you know who she is? If anything, she'll be looking after me!"

"Guys," Liz interrupts. "What was the square-up about earlier on today?"

"It wasn't a square-up, hen," laughs Tam as he puts an arm around Moose's broad shoulders. "The boy only wanted my permission to ask you for your hand in marriage. That's all."

"I rushed everything the last time," Moose nods in agreement. "I just wanted to do things properly this time and your dad was going to be my safety net if anything went wrong."

The celebrations continue back stage as a handful of dedicated fans join Hell Freeze and Molten Rock for chats, photos and autographs. Liz spots the elderly lady she had recognised from the audience.

"You are trying to think where you know us from, aren't you, my love?" the lady asks Liz.

"I am so sorry," Liz replies. "I have a dreadful mind for putting faces to names."

"My name is Judy and this is my daughter Liza," the lady tells Liz. "We have been massive fans of yours since we first heard you play at the small, local venues. The last time we saw you play was at your farewell gig."

"Oh my God," Liz gasps as the penny drops as she remembers the lady who was looking at her with pity at the farewell gig. "I saw you!"

"I really wanted to cuddle you and take you home with me along with the boy Angel," replies Judy. "I really felt for you and the boys, more especially you."

"I tell you," says Liz as her eyes fill with tears and that memory floods back to her. "I could REALLY have been doing with that cuddle. I really needed somebody to tell me everything was going to be alright but I had literally nowhere to turn."

"Well I am glad to see you have become such a strong woman and that the boys are doing well too," smiles Judy. "You even got your man back."

"I did," beams Liz. "I won't let him get away this time!"

Just then, somebody else catches Liz's attention. It is Phil Bryan of Molten Rock and he is accompanied by who Liz imagines is his current wife or partner. He smiles as he realises who Liz is.

"Welcome back, kiddo," Bryan smiles. "You've grown up since I last saw you. Please meet my wife Susan."

"Good to see you again, Mr Bryan," says Liz. She smiles warmly and is civil even though her last impression of him was not good. "Good to meet you Susan."

It was the night of the gig when Molten Rock had made their surprise appearance on stage with Hell Freeze before they had hit the big time. As it turned out, Rick Hammer had pulled said stunt because he and his bandmates saw potential in Hell Freeze and they wanted them to tour with them as their support act, an invitation which the band had accepted without hesitation.

The backstage celebrations continued as the two bands partied and enjoyed drinks. 16-year-old Liz was accompanied by Bryan's then fiancee Miranda Brown. Liz looked at Miranda with awe. She was a tall, stunning woman who worked as an actress and model and she would soon marry a musician who played for one of the most successful rock bands of all time. It was midnight and Bryan called Miranda over as they were going home. Miranda kissed Liz goodbye, they exchanged phone numbers and Miranda asked Liz to keep in touch. Papa Joe put an arm around Liz's shoulders and guided her out to his car but not before Moose noticed that Liz was crying.

Liz was in bed, unable to sleep, when she heard Debbie and her bandmates come home from their star-studded party in the very early hours of the morning. Moose and Angel chatted quietly as they got changed and into bed. Angel fell asleep almost instantly on the bottom bunk and Moose, who still worked as a fitness instructor and personal trainer, continued to read a physiology book with a torch on the top bunk. Liz looked up at Moose who happened to take his eyes off his book and was looking at her.

"Do you want to talk about it?" asked Moose, his voice hoarse after a busy week of teaching, performing and partying. "Sorry we couldn't take you with us. Did you not enjoy the gig and what about our tour with Molten Rock? Are you not up for it?"

Liz began to cry again as she climbed onto the top bunk beside Moose so she didn't disturb Angel. "It's nothing to do with the party," wept Liz as she lay on top of the duvet. "I knew I wouldn't be allowed to go because of my age and I was fine with that. Yes, I loved the gig. It was a buzz and, yes, of course I am up for the Molten Rock tour."

"What is it then?" pressed Moose as he put down his book.

"Did you see Phil Bryan's fiancee?" asked Liz.

"See her?" replied Moose excitedely. "Fuck yeah! If old Bryan doesn't want her, I'll do her. She'll be due a younger, fitter model soon no doubt."

"Really, Moose?" asked Liz, now unable to control her tears. "Put it this way. Would you do me?"

"Liz, have you gone mad?" Moose grimaced. "I would be on the sex offenders' register as a paedophile and behind bars in the blink of an eye! Even hardened criminals hate those vile beings."

"Moose," Liz whispered. "Miranda is two years younger than me! I feel so sick with worry thinking about her. That poor girl..."

Moose's expression was very different now and he looked disgusted because he now understood where young Liz was coming from. "Listen, baby," he told her. "We are going to make it big soon and you are going to see some very shady things in this business. The bigger we get the more shady, dirty things you are going to witness. If you want to bail out, now is your time."

"I can't," said Liz. "This is my job now and I don't want to let you guys down after all you've done for me."

"We're all here to protect you," Moose assured her as he gently squeezed her tiny hand. "Please remember that. Now try to get some sleep, baby. Tonight's gig was a tough one and you did really well...with everything."

Liz snaps back to reality as Amber congratulates her and her bandmates on their successful come-back.

"Amber," Liz smiles as she takes Moose's hand. "I have one more favour to ask you."

"Certainly, Liz," replies Amber. "What's that?"

Liz holds up her left hand to reveal her ring. "Will you do me the honour of being a bridesmaid at our wedding along with Angie, Debbie and Caitlin? You can even take pictures for your station website as you are responsible for getting Moose and I back together."

"Oh my God, Congratulations to both of you," cries Amber as she hugs Moose and Liz. "I would LOVE to be a bridesmaid for you. It would be an honour."

The past few months of hard work have, indeed, proved a success. Hell Freeze are back from retirement and their single "Demons" is Christmas number one for the year. Despite all their doubts and set-backs, the band have come full circle and are back to stay.